THE VESPUCCI PAPERS

By the same author

WAITING FOR A TIGER
THE TERRIBLE PICTURES

THE VESPUCCI PAPERS

by

BEN HEALEY

J. B. LIPPINCOTT COMPANY
Philadelphia and New York

U. S. Library of Congress Cataloging in Publication Data

Healey, Ben.
    The Vespucci papers.

    I. Title.
PZ4.H4343Ve [PS3558.E23]   813'.5'4   76-38406
ISBN–0–397–00776–0

Copyright © 1972 by Ben Healey
All rights reserved
Printed in the United States of America

All the characters in this book are fictitious, and no reference is intended to any living person or existing families.

Arturo's theories have no foundation in history as it is known at present, nor is there any record that Giuliano de' Medici ever made such extravagant gifts to Simonetta Vespucci. But, since he was an extremely wealthy and impulsive young man, neither is there any reason why he should not have done; and there is very little doubt that Sandro Botticelli must have painted at least one portrait of Simonetta for him.

Arturo Vespucci's script.

... ES USFZ CL VZMVOLI UPS UIEZ QNO ZUUZTTS GCZMTI QOCNOZLI RC ZEEZEE LSNNZ UIEH TSO HZAAO 1478 TCS ZLLO TIHI NZ MIFDS TO EOMILSDDZ ...

Simone's first transcription showing the two words (underlined) which finally gave her the solution.

CHAPTER ONE

Mr Harcourt d'Espinal pushed back his chair from the breakfast table, a chair which looked already as if it was too frail and exquisite to bear his considerable weight, and stared distastefully at the two letters. They lay side by side, white and virginal in their apparent innocence; but there was a grim set to d'Espinal's lips, an altogether untypical frown lying dark and straight across the habitually quizzical and benevolent eyebrows. Both were addressed from Paris. One, on slightly over-expensive paper, and typed as only Gregor could mishandle a typewriter when the matter was too delicate for the eyes of his secretary; and the other under the crest of the Hotel Georges Cinq written in a damnably firm, crisp and self-certain feminine hand. The hand of a woman who wrote with a purpose.

Like a big cat cautiously investigating some suspicious object with its paw he stretched out one finger to push them aside. There was no doubt, he considered, that Gregor was in a twitter; the very devil of a twitter. And then he said aloud, 'This is damned nonsense,' and took up the first of them again firmly.

Gregor wrote:

'My dear Harcourt; you will forgive my misfortunes with this abominable machine, but this affair is one which I feel deeply should be contained most strictly between ourselves.

The situation is this. Yesterday our colleague Hakim received a visitation. One notably interesting as to her person and though a *soupçon* over-businesslike—which is a disaster in a woman—indubitably a lady. The conversation was to the effect that she wished to know how far our friend's interest might extend in the matter of an hitherto unknown portrait by a certain Maestro of the late fifteenth century, Florentine; and she proposed a value which our good Hakim confesses caused his blood to freeze. Which must have been a sufficiently entrancing achievement...

She spoke further of that artist, the Sublime One, who is reputed in a moment of religion to have burned many of his more profane or carnal labours—the expression always enchants me, my dear fellow; does it not you?—and the indication appears that this subject is claimed to be a work which, as one might say, somehow escaped the burning fiery furnace...

Our excellent Hakim, with that modesty which is his greatest charm, replied that he was merely the poorest of dealers and he could not presume to envisage money of such shocking magnitude. To this the visitation answered by speaking of your name and enquiring kindly of your present residence; and she mentioned in passing the matter of a small Correggio study, which was sold to the wife of a Greek and then came out so unhappily to be not a little Correggio after all. You recollect the occasion? Poor Hakim confesses that he suffered a distinct feeling, a *frisson*. And we all know how spiteful Greek millionaires can be, how difficult it often is to persuade them that even the greatest expert can sometimes slip into an innocent, simple mistake...

How this visitation acquired that information she did not explain and, as ever, our good Hakim was too much a gentleman to ask. But she announced that she would be passing on to London that day, and she would desire to meet you herself. Hakim has expressed the wish that our ever kindly Lord might see fit to arrange something inexpressibly severe for her; but one feels that is not to be. Therefore I have no doubt that with your magnificent generosity towards all the ladies you will hasten to do everything you can to assure her contentment. Also it might be wise...

Accept, my dear Harcourt, our expressions of most profound respect...'

D'Espinal gazed across the quiet, peaceful room with its subdued colourings, at a beautiful little early Italian Madonna and Child placed with precise care on the dull ivory wall between tall windows hung with muted green drapes. It was a forgery of course. Indeed he knew and had the greatest regard for the man who had painted it barely six months before. It was genius in its way; to so capture the very soul of devotion. The combination of soft blues and glowing crimson, the half seen background of an eternally golden afternoon in Tuscany, never failed to satisfy him; and when at last the time came for him to part with the picture, to one enthusiastic but somewhat ill-informed collector who was already showing interest, he would do so with real regret however much he needed the money.

But this morning its colour seemed to be ever so slightly harsh, the landscape a little less serene, and even the modelling of the robe a trifle clumsy for a genuine Matteo di Giovanni ... It was a risky trade, a damned deceptive risky trade, he thought, and reached out for the other letter; taking it up as gingerly as if it were a viper.

It started:

'Dear Mr Harcourt d'Espinal; I fear you will not know of me although we have at least one common friend in Mrs Aristide (Tina) Drikos, and an interest shared by all three of us in Italian Renaissance painting—although I would not dare claim to be such an expert as yourself...'

D'Espinal whispered something under his breath.

'I happened to meet Tina only a few weeks ago and you will be interested, perhaps even a little amused, to hear that she is most concerned about the authenticity of a reputed Correggio study which she purchased—in circumstances of great secrecy one gathers—in Paris last summer. It *really* is quite a comedy. As you might guess the thing now appears to be merely a clever forgery, and poor Tina is torn between a very natural desire to expose the fraud and an equally natural fear of her husband's rage if he discovers that she was so simply taken in; and with such immense effrontery. For the present at least he remains in happy ignorance, but one can never be quite sure of what might happen next where Tina is concerned...

However, I must not waste your time on social chatter, pleasant as it may be. I am writing on behalf of my aunt, Mrs Judith Teestock, of Isola San Giorgio Piccolo, Venice—who is well known for her charitable interests in the outer islands and with whom I have the privilege of working as secretary and companion. She wishes to ask whether we might persuade you to visit us here for a week or so in the near future? You must of course have many calls on your time; but I can promise that your journey will not be wasted, since we should like you to examine what is undoubtedly an hitherto unknown Botticelli and obviously a work of quite extraordinary importance. It is no less than a portrait of Simonetta Vespucci, painted shortly before her death for her lover Giuliano de' Medici, the younger brother of Lorenzo the Magnificent.'

'Dear God,' d'Espinal breathed. 'The damned woman takes one's breath away.'
She went on:

'I need hardly say that we must ask you to keep the very strictest confidence. If you will forgive the little joke none of us would like Tina Drikos, for instance, to come running to Venice looking for another bargain; or perhaps for the person who sold her that fraudulent Correggio at such an outrageous price...

We shall hope to see you, and suggest May 12 as the most convenient date. But by the time you receive this letter I shall be in London myself, and I suggest we meet and discuss the whole matter more fully. I feel sure you will be interested ... Yours most sincerely, Emilia Pentecost.'

D'Espinal closed his eyes for a long moment, his lips moving silently as if in some kind of secret prayer, and then opened them again to stare thoughtfully at the big bookcase filling one entire wall of the quiet green and ivory room. 'Simonetta, the divine mistress; the tragic girl,' he murmured, and then got up suddenly to take out one big and another smaller volume. It took him only a few seconds to find what he wanted and he read 'Simonetta Vespucci, born Cattaneo in or near Genoa 1453. Married Marco di Piero Vespucci, cousin to Amerigo Vespucci the merchant-navigator, at the age of sixteen; or as some say, thirteen ... Became known to Sandro Botticelli in Florence who painted what is thought to be the one extant portrait of her and later immortalized her in the "Primavera" and the "Birth of Venus" (both executed for the Medici) and in the "Venus and Mars" for the Vespucci family. Mistress of Giuliano de' Medici, who rode under her banner in the Great Tournament of Florence, 1475. Died 1476, aged twenty-three, and buried in the Church of All Saints, Florence; when the entire city observed a solemn day of mourning in her honour. Lorenzo de' Medici himself wrote of her, "It seemed impossible that she was loved by so many men without jealousy and praised by so many women without envy."'

'So,' d'Espinal breathed, 'our Miss Pentecost reaches high.'

He flipped open the bigger book, ran his finger down the index and then riffled back to a full page plate, studying it critically. 'So,' he repeated, 'the only known portrait by Botticelli, and there is a query even to that, is at present in the Kunstinstitut, Frankfurt-am-Main. Nor,' he added, 'is that a very prepossessing likeness. But is there another one? Can there be?'

'What has the woman got?' he asked, staring through the window at a distant view over Richmond Park; a drift of soft new grass and a herd of deer cropping peacefully, the trees tossing up their new young leaves like fountains of green spray and a glittering blue and silver April sky. Seen through the glass it looked as quiet and fragile as a soap bubble; and he knew that like a soap bubble it might vanish at a touch along with his leisured and pleasant, if amiably dishonest, life. A touch from this confounded mysterious Miss Pentecost; who could and clearly would make all the trouble in the world over that little Correggio.

He said explosively, 'Damnation!' But then whispered, 'An unknown Botticelli. In mere mercantile terms at least a million pounds; perhaps three million dollars...' For a time again he brooded heavily, studying the cool English pastoral beyond the window; thinking of the colours of Venice. 'Very well, Miss Pentecost,' he announced at last, 'I shall come. But not on the twelfth. A week before, I think. A week in which to find out for myself what you're up to, dear lady.' Harcourt d'Espinal always had a nice sense of the dramatic; almost as nice as his sense of Italian Renaissance painting.

Simone Greenwood looked doubtfully across the desk at her visitor; the tailored suit and neat hat, the calm pale face with very little make-up and dark, rather fine eyes. Thirty-five perhaps, and professional looking. Quiet, and very friendly. But there was no doubt that Miss Pentecost was a managing sort of personality; she would want to have things her own way.

Simone was wearing heavy, horn-rimmed glasses. They magnified her grey eyes a little, but they were slightly comic with her shining tawny blonde hair, and they did not make her look any older nor more dignified. Rather in fact they made one feel that she had stolen her mother's spectacles for some private fancy of her own; perhaps a determined attempt to seem severe and important.

At this moment she did not much like her visitor's questions. They sounded as if Miss Pentecost was trying to fish for her qualifications; and that really was a trifle impudent. It was probably her appearance again. She simply did not look like historical research. She ought to wear dark brown clothes, get her hair cut in a Hampstead fringe, and put at least another ten years on her age. But she had left that too late now, and for the present at least one had to be polite to prospective clients; she needed them too badly. A little defensively, which made her seem younger still, she answered, 'I started it when I came down from college. I thought there was a demand for it. And I've a sort of knack for digging out obscure information.'

'It must be fascinating,' Miss Pentecost said. 'Like a detective in history.'

Simone stared at her. 'Mostly it's grubbing around in old books.'

Miss Pentecost took in the small, modest office. 'And not very successful,' she thought, wondering briefly if there was a man in the background somewhere. The girl was not wearing a ring but, as they had always realized, it was quite possible and it might be a complication; she was an attractive creature and her air of slight hesitation could well have an irresistible attraction to perhaps the rather tiresomely protective type. Miss Pentecost considered that for a moment and then asked, 'Miss Greenwood, have you any ties? I mean would you be free to come to Venice? Perhaps for some time.'

Simone did not answer at once, thinking that Miss Pentecost could not possibly guess how free she was, or how much time she had. But she said cautiously, 'It would rather depend on what for. And how long.'

'How long?' Miss Pentecost smiled at her. 'You could decide that for yourself. And as to what for...' She leaned forward slightly. 'I think we can offer you something really exciting in research; one might even call it startling. If you're interested.' She paused again, watching Simone, and then went on, 'We should be more than grateful. If only for the princess. She's so set on it.'

'We?' Simone asked. 'And the princess? It sounds exotic.'

'Princess Kodaly. It's a Hungarian title; from her second marriage.' Miss Pentecost raised one shoulder and dismissed that easily. 'That doesn't matter. It's the first husband who will interest you ... His name was Arturo Vespucci.'

Simone repeated, 'Vespucci?' She took off her glasses, examined them carefully and put them on again to gaze at Miss Pentecost. 'Yes?' she asked.

'He was an extraordinary man. Very wealthy; very

determined. And he was fascinated by the Vespucci of Florence, the old Vespucci; particularly Simonetta. You know of them, of course?'

'A certain amount.'

'A great deal, I'm sure. As much as can be known. Except perhaps for Arturo Vespucci's discoveries.' Miss Pentecost paused carefully. She seemed to be listening to the snore of the London traffic in Earl's Court Road outside the little office, before going on, 'He did a lot of research himself. And when he died he left a great many notes; most of them written in a kind of private shorthand.'

Simone did not answer for a time, cautiously checking her sudden excitement. 'You mean you want me? To put them in order?'

'Rather more than that. The princess hopes you'll write a book on them afterwards. The book poor Arturo himself intended to write before he died so suddenly. You see now why one asked you if you are free. It's a lot of work.'

'It is,' Simone agreed. She took a deep breath, still determined to keep quite calm. 'It is indeed.'

'It should be interesting, too. Arturo had some unusual ideas. He was convinced there ought to be at least one more portrait of Simonetta Vespucci in existence. And he thought there might have been something peculiar about her death.'

Behind the big glasses Simone's eyes widened suddenly. 'He what?' she asked. She was not sure she liked that; it sounded like pure sensationalism. 'It's doubtful, you know. After five hundred years nothing's ever quite certain, but Simonetta's supposed to have died of consumption and nobody's ever suggested anything else. If it's some idea of another of these fantastic Renaissance poisons ... They're just an eighteenth-century legend. They simply didn't exist.'

'Of course not.' Miss Pentecost sounded slightly impatient. 'But Arturo was right about one thing, about the picture. There was another portrait of Simonetta Vespucci; and he found it. He considered that it was painted for Giuliano de' Medici; by Botticelli. I don't need to tell you what that means.'

'No,' Simone agreed, 'you don't.' She straightened the blotting pad on her desk carefully, trying still to appear non-committal. The whole thing was impossible; the sort of thing all research workers dreamed of while knowing that it could never happen. She murmured, 'It would be the discovery of the century.'

'Rather more than that, I should think ... Let me put it all quite simply. Princess Kodaly has this picture in her possession along with a mass of material left by her first husband. He claimed the picture is an unknown Botticelli, but the experts would probably argue about that; perhaps for years. The princess herself says that Arturo's notes will explain how he discovered it and prove its authenticity. And she would like you to come out to Venice to decipher and then publish them as a memorial to him. You would be doing her a very great favour; she understands that; and ...' Miss Pentecost smiled again, 'she is an extremely wealthy woman. One has to be businesslike; it could be the chance of a lifetime, Miss Greenwood.'

Simone frowned slightly before answering. 'Yes. That's what I find so puzzling.' She asked flatly, 'Why me? I'm not all that well known, and there are dozens of historical research workers in Italy, brilliant people. Why doesn't the princess go to one of those?'

'You have a quick mind.' And some time, Miss Pentecost thought, it might be too quick... 'It's quite simple. She doesn't like them; neither did Arturo. He was an amateur. They thought he was a crank and a charlatan; and they said so. The princess has never forgiven it.' Miss Pentecost paused again and then added carefully, 'There is another point. You appear to fascinate her. After all, you're a Vespucci yourself.'

Simone looked startled and very young; embarrassed and even slightly aggressive. 'That's nonsense. I never claimed that. It's impossible.'

'But your grandmother was Simonetta. And her maiden name was Vespucci.'

'There must be dozens of men called Henry Tudor around,' Simone answered tartly. 'But they don't claim to be descendants of King Henry the Eighth ... I suppose it was that magazine write-up?'

Although careful not to show it Miss Pentecost was amused. '*The Ladies' Bazaar*,' she agreed, 'January this year. The princess studies most of the women's journals; it's quite a habit with her. She is English, of course; I didn't say. And when she saw the article about you and your work, and the photograph, she made up her mind at once. She's like that, you know.'

'We'd better get this clear,' Simone said. 'When *The Ladies' Bazaar* asked to do that piece about me in their series on women in careers I just thought it could be a sort of advertisement.'

'And so it was. The princess talked of nothing else for days.'

'Not the kind I want. I did tell them my grandmother's name was Simonetta Vespucci; which was silly of me. But I didn't imagine they'd build it up like that. And I certainly didn't realize they were going to mess about with my photograph. I was very angry about it, and I still am. I happen to think the truth's rather important. In my trade I must.'

So earnest, Miss Pentecost thought, really rather a little prig; and that might be dangerous too. She said, 'Of course. But there is one point. The princess may or may not think that you're a descendant of the Vespucci. I quite agree it's almost impossible myself. But she's absolutely convinced that you must be some distant connection of her first husband. I really wouldn't disappoint her about that if I were you.'

'I haven't said I'm coming yet.'

'We hope you will.' Miss Pentecost got up and took her handbag and gloves. 'Don't decide too quickly. Sleep on it. And then let's have dinner together tomorrow. But I shall do my best to persuade you. Becky Kodaly will never forgive me if I don't; and Aunt Judith will be bitterly disappointed. And it's unkind to disappoint her, she does so much good herself. We live on one of the small private islands in the Lagoon; San Giorgio Piccolo. I promise you'll love it; it's just a perfect little garden to itself, and the house is delightful. If you wanted to you could work there in preference to the Ca' Vespucci—that's the princess's place in Venice—which is rather ancient and gloomy.'

'You make it sound very tempting,' Simone murmured.

'I intend to,' Miss Pentecost answered gaily. 'I'll pick you up tomorrow night about seven and we'll have a gorgeous meal somewhere.'

Opening the door for her Simone watched her start down the flight of dark brown stairs, thinking of the contrast between this tired old apartment house and that island, whatever it was; Little Saint George. She almost said then, 'Yes, I'll come,' but Miss Pentecost stopped suddenly and looked back up at her. 'By the way,' she asked, 'have you ever met a man named d'Espinal? Harcourt d'Espinal?'

Simone considered it carefully. 'I don't think so. No. With a name like that you'd be sure to remember. Why?'

'It doesn't matter. He's a friend of Aunt Judith's and I thought if you knew him he might tell you about her.'

'When would you want me to come?' Simone asked suddenly.

'You'll need time to make your arrangements here,' Miss Pentecost said. 'About the beginning of May?' She nodded, smiled again, and went on; while Simone listened to her shoes echoing in the quietness for a minute and then turned back into the office.

It seemed to be curiously silent and vaguely depressing now and Simone said, 'If I don't go I shall spend the rest of my life wondering what it was all about. But there's something very odd there. And why me?' She frowned across at the filing cabinet as if that could give her the answer, then opened it to take out a copy of a glossy women's journal; turning over the pages and, like d'Espinal, stopping to look at a portrait with her head tilted slightly to one side. This time it was of herself. But of herself so posed and so carefully retouched that you could see in it an unmistakable likeness to a face in one of the most famous pictures in the world; the face of a girl who had died five hundred years ago at the age of twenty-three.

CHAPTER TWO

D'Espinal stepped ashore from the airways launch at San Marco into a total effect of noise, colour and glitter. Sunlight flashing off the green water, a moving pattern of crowded ferry boats, black gondolas and polished launches, across the Grand Canal the gleaming domes of the Church of the Salute against a vivid sky, and on the white marble pavement this side the gaudy brilliance of flower stalls and silks and trinket salesmen; and an eddying chattering crowd like a restless kaleidoscope. In London only a little over two hours ago it had been raining dourly. But here the summer was already in full bloom and out over the lagoon you could see that curious iridescent shimmer which always made him think, a little fancifully, that Venice was a city encased at the heart of a vast, pale blue opal.

He walked majestically into the terminal building to claim his baggage, and there again was the young woman who had been sitting across the aisle from him in the aircraft. She had then been reading a severe looking book and wearing large heavy spectacles, but even so he had been haunted for a while by a sort of elusive recognition; a feeling that although he did not know this girl herself he had at some time known someone very like her. Seeing her now without the glasses the impression was even stronger. He was certain that he knew the warm blonde hair and arched eyebrows, the slightly wide set eyes and half smiling mouth. It was a picture somewhere. Then it struck him quite clearly. For a moment the flustered babel of the air terminal seemed to die away, while he stared at a face which Sandro Botticelli might have painted. He murmured, 'Dear Lord God...' lost for a moment in another age.

She did not notice d'Espinal. She was looking past him, and she smiled suddenly, raised one hand and said clearly, 'Hallo, Miss Pentecost.'

At that he jolted unpleasantly back to the present. The agitation of this place, the fret of people now impatient to get to their journey's end, the polyglot chatter all closed in around him again and he turned himself to see Miss Pentecost there, as surprised as he was; and a damned unwelcome surprise, he thought. He had not bargained on the woman realizing that he was in Venice already, a week early; he was no less put out than she appeared to be and he wondered briefly what one should do now, whether to outface the devil and salute her like a gentleman and so find out at once who this girl was, or to affect to be invisible.

Miss Pentecost herself settled it. She hesitated for the fraction of a second and then brushed past him quickly; he heard her say, 'It's nice to see you, did you have a good flight?' There was a burly dark-skinned fellow with her, wearing blue trousers and a nautical jacket rather as if he had put them on specially for the occasion, and she went on, 'Pietro will pick up your bags,' and turned her back on d'Espinal deliberately. One could not mistake the message and he stepped back with some relief while, almost hustling the girl away, she went on again, 'Our boat's at the Molo; it's a little walk.'

D'Espinal watched them disappear into the crowd before he nodded absently to a porter, gave the man his baggage check and said, 'A taxi, if you please; to the gallery of Signor Paolo Raffaele on the Rio della Toletta, the Accademia.' And then for once oblivious to the glittering spectacle of one of the most colourful water highways in the world, he sat in the stern of the taxi boat brooding heavily as they cruised up the Grand Canal and under the great shadow of the Accademia Bridge. He watched the green water sliding past when they slowed down and turned into a narrow opening between tall buildings, while the noise and movement behind them died away into the secret quietness of the unknown Venice, silent backwaters, ancient sun-bleached stone and soft red brick, where you slipped back three centuries in as many minutes. But he had no eyes for it this time. He was puzzled and perturbed; somewhere in this business already he could smell wickedness.

Paolo Raffaele's gallery lay at the end of a small, silent canal; a surprising garden with gravelled walks and trees and feathery climbing shrubs. The afternoon sunlight dappled a group of statuary and a rather disapproving portrait bust of one of the Doges; and, half hidden by the greenery, a pair of marble lions looked out with faint permanent surprise as if somehow they had got left there by mistake. To the left was a glazed arcade where the colour of pictures and the glint of their frames could just be seen through the glass, and facing the gate an old timber and stone dwelling; an open fronted studio workshop, a flight of steps going up to a wide balcony with low browed, red tiled eaves hanging far out over it. D'Espinal always thought it was such a scene as Guardi might have lived in and painted, even to the very old man working there in the shade.

His brown face wrinkled with concentration he was humming gently between his teeth while gilding a small wooden cherub, and d'Espinal watched him for a moment before saying, 'Well, Andreas?' A slow, wide grin of recognition cracked the wrinkled face and he whispered, 'So you have come. Now we shall have an opera again.' The bright, naughty little eyes glinted mischievously. 'The girl has put a room ready for you. She is dreaming that maybe this time you will at last seduce her before it gets too late.'

'How old is she now?' d'Espinal asked. 'Seventy-two? You should be ashamed.' It was an ancient joke but Andreas chuckled happily as d'Espinal turned to climb the steps. The girl was already waiting at the top of them, not so elderly by ten years as the old man but almost as dark, and she announced, 'I heard that. You may tell that wicked one that the day they take him to San Michele with a priest I will dance for his funeral.'

'You do not improve, Annunzietta,' d'Espinal told her sadly. 'But you are as beautiful as ever. I still say that Michelangelo should have painted you.' This too was part of the ritual and the old woman cackled appreciatively and reached out for his suitcase. 'No, 'Etta,' he said, 'I shall carry it in myself. Is the padrone awake?'

Paolo Raffaele came out quietly. He was not quite

so old as the other two and indeed, as d'Espinal knew, they both thought of him as a young man; it was hard to say who looked after which in this establishment. He had a shock of white hair, old fashioned gold-rimmed spectacles perched habitually askew on his nose, and a mild scholarly face which curiously belied the amusement and the occasional sardonic glint in his eyes. 'Well, Harcourt,' he asked. 'How long is it?'

'Three years; four years.' D'Espinal studied him with real affection, and looked at the bleached silvery timbers of the balcony, the old yellow cane chairs and the four or five well fed cats dozing in the shade. He said softly, 'Nothing changes, Paolo.'

'A few years older. And not so much wiser. Come and sit down.' Paolo nudged one of the animals out of a chair. 'That is Benvenuto Cellini; a wicked fellow. And there is Isabella d'Este. Cesare Borgia for the moment appears to be away from home ... How is it with you, Harcourt? You look prosperous.'

D'Espinal sat down, the chair creaking a little. 'Prosperous? I'm almost destitute. I've thought even of entering a monastery.'

'In which case the good brothers would need to have a care for their pictures. And you come here instead. Does one ask why?'

'Paolo!' He sounded reproachful. 'Must you impute to me such base motives?'

'But my dear fellow, why not? What are friends for if one does not use them? And I fancy that old Andreas and Annunzietta rather suspect you're about some business.'

The big man brooded heavily for a moment. 'I'm in a pickle, Paolo, the devil of a pickle. I need your help; and knowledge. I remember you once said that you could hear the whispers of Venice floating along the canals.'

'To be precise, Annunzietta can.'

D'Espinal paused thoughtfully, watching the cats, and then said, 'I have a very strange tale to unfold. And I have just seen Simonetta Vespucci.' Paolo stared at him and he added, 'Arriving in a perfectly prosaic aeroplane from London and being whisked away before one could speak or look. A tantalizing, half seen, half remembered resemblance. But for one moment in an impossible place, surrounded by banality, a quite ordinary young woman suddenly became one of Sandro Botticelli's girls. It was a very strange experience.' He went on to describe it at some length.

Paolo listened patiently and asked at last, 'Why should it be? A simple likeness is common enough. You can see women who might have been Titian's models still walking in the Merceria. My own late dear wife at one time bore a startling likeness to the Madonna of the Rose Arbor. It was that fact which caused me later to have my first doubts about religion.'

'In this case,' d'Espinal said, 'I begin to see a mystery. And, unless my instinct fails me, a pretty piece of devilment. There's villainy afoot, old friend, and damned tricky female villainy at that.' For a time he sat very still, his eyes half closed and pouting slightly, while Paolo watched him with a sort of kindly cynicism until he demanded, 'Tell me, have you ever heard that there is a lost Botticelli, one of those paintings he is supposed to have burned, here in Venice?'

'A Botticelli?' Paolo shook his head gently. 'I've heard of the Kodaly picture, of course. It is a forgery.'

'So it does exist? Have you seen it?'

'As one understands nobody in Venice has seen it. Except the Kodaly servants perhaps.'

'Then how do you know it's a forgery?'

'My dear Harcourt, everyone knows. Because it must be. There's no such thing as a lost Botticelli. And if there were would any woman in her senses keep it hidden away?'

'She might,' d'Espinal answered softly, 'if her own title to it were doubtful. And I know that two people at least have seen it; two ladies of impeccable gentility. They have no doubt whatever.'

'Ladies,' Paolo observed, 'are not always reliable.'

'You have a somewhat clouded view of the sex. For my part I'm convinced there's something here; it's a very odd business. And almost certainly this other young woman who appeared today is involved.' He brooded again for a time, staring down at the quiet, gold and green garden. 'I see as through a glass, darkly,' he murmured. 'As yet I have been told nothing in so many words, but I have no doubt that they are planning quietly to steal this picture. In which nefarious enterprise I too am to be enrolled.'

Paolo's eyebrows rose slightly. He asked, 'Willingly? Or otherwise?'

'This Emilia Pentecost,' d'Espinal muttered. 'I will tell you everything, precisely as it happened.' While he talked Paolo lazily stroked the cat, Benvenuto Cellini, apparently listening rather to its deep hoarse purr than to d'Espinal himself, only smiling faintly when he finished. 'In the upshot I gave the woman a damnably expensive lunch during which it was remarkable how little was said and how much hinted. Except I was told that my professional services were required; I surmise that I am expected to sell it ... And I had already decided that it might be wise to arrive here a few days early to make my own plans.'

'And what are they?'

D'Espinal looked at him from under his eyelids. 'If that picture is a Botticelli ... What do you think?' He went on quickly, 'I shall not involve you; I have my standards, such as they are. But in any case I'm inquisitive. I want to find out, Paolo. Don't you?'

Paolo thought about that carefully before he answered, 'If there is a Botticelli; yes. I think perhaps I do.'

'So...' d'Espinal breathed. 'What can you tell me about this Princess Kodaly?'

'No more than all Venice knows. Her first husband was disliked here, and her second was an undesirable. She herself is not accepted; it is possible to live for many years in Venice, you know, and still be a stranger. She is said to drink, which is deplorable but not necessarily fatal. Signora Messina-Silvestro disapproves of her, which is. She does not go to church and gives nothing to charity; and that is a mistake. And she employs a lady's maid who appears to take more upon herself than she should.'

'Poor woman,' d'Espinal murmured. He brooded again for a time and added, 'I don't care for it, old friend. I am a man of sensitivity and I can feel a pricking in my thumbs ... Arturo Vespucci, the first husband; why was he not liked?'

'There was a minor, silly affair. Unlike you he was

not a man of sensitivity,' Paolo said gently. 'He made one foolish mistake and then refused to correct it. When they came to Venice, in the late fifties I think, he bought an old place off the Rio della Fava. It had always been known as the Ca' Fava; and he changed its name to the Ca' Vespucci.'

'Is that all? As simple as that?'

'What is simple? He was foolish enough to tell Signora Messina-Silvestro to mind her own business. And she is not a lady to take such advice lightly. It is said of her that when her own husband lay dying his last words were, "Lord, now lettest thou thy servant depart in peace".'

'Did you know Arturo Vespucci?' d'Espinal demanded a little impatiently.

'He came here occasionally. He was knowledgeable and enthusiastic. Perhaps too much so.'

'Tell me, Paolo; you are a scholar so would you say that he was? And would you say that he was capable, psychologically capable as it were, of tracing and finding an unknown Botticelli? Did he have the intuition?'

'Again what is a scholar? I would say that he was superficial. And as for the picture...' The old man shrugged. 'I am absolutely certain that he was quite capable of creating a theory and then persuading himself that the evidence supported it. In my reading Arturo Vespucci was one who would have to prove himself right at any cost.'

Except for Andreas singing softly to himself below it was very quiet. The sun was going down and the garden fading to bosky green, although the ancient red brick building across the canal was still glowing in soft warm rose. A black gondola swayed across and they could hear the thin ripple of the water as it passed. The cat named Isabella d'Este got up and stretched ready for the evening's business; she stalked off inside and one by one the others followed her.

Paolo said, "'Etta will be calling us in soon; she is preparing quite a feast,' but he appeared still to be thinking of Arturo Vespucci. 'There is one thing, perhaps. He was a close friend of old Rutilio Lenardi of the Accademia Library. Lenardi was a very learned man; and he did not suffer fools gladly. It is possible that he found something in Vespucci which the rest of us were too busy to notice.'

'So there you have it. Let us go and talk to this Lenardi.'

'You would find it difficult,' Paolo answered dryly. 'He died before Vespucci himself.'

D'Espinal grunted, sitting with his chin sunk on his chest and watching Andreas, another cat pacing behind him, walk slowly across the garden to close the wrought iron gates on to the canal. 'Simonetta dead these five hundred years,' he muttered, 'Vespucci dead and Lenardi dead. And the second husband too, I understand.'

'Prince Stefan Kodaly. A ski-jumping accident in the Tyrol as I heard. He can be discounted; he was merely a flashy rogue.'

'But he too is dead. Do I fancy there is starting to be a graveyard smell about this thing?' d'Espinal asked heavily. 'I shall go with Annunzietta to Mass tomorrow.'

Sitting on the patio with Mrs Teestock, Simone listened to Miss Pentecost playing the piano in the room behind them. It sounded like a Scarlatti pastorale—at least it should have been in this place—and rather fancifully she imagined the rippling, airy notes flickering like the early fire flies which were now starting to glint and flash over the shadowy garden. She thought of them dancing away over the dark water, barely moving and just gleaming with reflected stars, towards the distant lights of Venice laid out like a string of jewels on almost black velvet.

Mrs Teestock said, 'We're very quiet here. I sometimes fancy that Emilia finds it too quiet.'

She was about sixty. In her younger days she would have been described as a handsome woman; and she still was, but now with some of the firm chiselling a little rubbed down. A type which was once the backbone of English village life—or perhaps of Indian, Simone suspected shrewdly—now expatriated and just slightly out of date; good manners because they were expected of one, behaviour and social responsibility which were simply the duties of one's position. She was clearly the padrona of this little island and the staff Simone had seen so far—the smiling young maid who had served dinner, Pietro the boatman and Mrs Pietro the cook—obviously loved her.

But however carefully concealed it might be you could catch an unmistakable hint of anxiety. Not much, yet enough to make Simone uneasy; as if she herself had brought something unpredictable with her. For something to say she murmured, 'Coming across from Venice Miss Pentecost was telling me that you do a lot of good work here.'

'We try. But there's so much needed; some of the

outer islands are terribly poor, you know. There's always room for far more than I can afford. And money seems to be worth less every day.'

'Does the princess help you?' Simone asked.

It was a simple question and perfectly innocent but Mrs Teestock seemed to close up suddenly; there was a sharp, uncomfortable little silence for a moment before she said, 'The princess has her own point of view.' She turned round in her chair, looking back into the room, and called, 'Emilia, are you coming out?'

The piano stopped and Miss Pentecost's long shadow fell across the pavement in the light from the french windows. She was wearing an oddly barbaric dress in dull greens and blues, with her hair now coiled round her head like a dark coronet; impressive in a way, Simone thought, but too operatic, she looked something like Lady Macbeth. She asked, 'Well, you two; how are you getting on?'

Simone was politely non-committal, but Mrs Teestock smiled up at the other woman and answered, 'Why, Emilia, what a silly question. We're getting on famously; was there ever any doubt of it?'

'Tell me about the princess,' Simone said.

'As to that, my dear...' Mrs Teestock leaned forward earnestly. 'I do think people should always be left to form their own first impressions. It's so misleading to see someone through another person's eyes. Becky is just a nice, kindly, very homely woman.'

'And you'll be meeting her tomorrow,' Miss Pentecost finished.

'I feel rather as if I'm going to be under inspection.'

'She's far more likely to feel like that than you,' Miss Pentecost told her crisply, 'with everything she's been building up around you.'

'She wanted to come over and meet you today,' Mrs Teestock added. 'But we were quite firm. We said you must be allowed to get your breath back after the journey. My dear...' She was even more earnest. 'You're in a position to do a rather lonely woman a great kindness. I don't think you'll refuse; whatever you might think of the princess.'

'There's no question of refusing. Why should there be? It's only that I'm still wondering.' Simone broke off, watching a solitary boat with one yellow light at its masthead drifting past in the darkness and throwing a long, rippling reflection across the black water. She went on slowly, 'I asked a friend of mine in London, an art dealer, how much he thought an unknown Botticelli might be worth.'

Miss Pentecost seemed to freeze suddenly. She demanded, 'You did what?'

Simone stared at her and then at Mrs Teestock. 'Shouldn't I have done? I'm sorry. I didn't realize it was a secret.'

'It isn't,' Mrs Teestock cut in quickly. 'Of course not. Everyone in Venice knows about it. What did he say?'

'He laughed. He said there's no such animal. But if there were it could be anything. A million pounds or even more.'

'It's a rather unnecessary speculation.' Miss Pentecost appeared to have relaxed again. 'Becky wouldn't dream of selling it.'

'You see,' Mrs Teestock explained gently, 'none of us has ever thought of it in those terms. To us it isn't merely so much money; it's a very beautiful picture, perhaps with a rather strange history. And we hope you can tell us what that is.'

'All the same...' Miss Pentecost was watching Simone—her hair darker now, almost coppery in the warm light, her face and shoulders and dress half luminous against the shadowy blue background of the garden—thinking that you really could imagine a resemblance, it was extraordinary. 'All the same I think Miss Greenwood ought to be quite businesslike. When you consider the connection with Amerigo Vespucci and the interest there'll be in America...'

Simone saw Mrs Teestock glance at Emilia uneasily. She wondered what the relationship between the two really was, whether there was even a hint of Lesbian possessiveness in it, and then discarded the idea immediately; it was out of character for both. More likely Miss Pentecost was simply what she called herself; the niece-companion-secretary. But the one who was taking control; the more determined personality of the two. It did not matter much, Simone told herself, it was making mysteries where none existed, and she got up and said, 'Do you mind if I go to bed? It's been a rather long day.'

'My dear, of course.' Mrs Teestock pushed herself up too. 'I always think it's terribly exhausting travelling by aeroplane. I'll come along to see you've got everything you want.'

Miss Pentecost watched them leave, then took a cigarette out of the box on the table, lit it thoughtfully and went down the shallow steps into the garden, walking slowly across towards the landing stage, her blue and green dress fading into the dark. There was a little breeze coming up and the water rippled and splashed uneasily as she stood looking across at the shimmering, flickering lights of Venice; to her like a vast ship in the blackness, a ship that never got anywhere. She tossed her cigarette over the balustrade, heard it die with a sharp little hiss, and turned to stare back at the long low house, the squat tower half hidden by cypresses at one end where she had her studio and the stucco and timber vine pergola, watching the lighted window which was Simone's room.

It was a bad start, she thought. That fat poseur appearing a week early and obviously interested in the girl; Simone herself the wrong type and Judith already realizing it. Yet they had always known there was a risk she might be and they had to have her, only Simone Greenwood and none other; mercenary or hard and they would have bargained with her, or a fool and she could be used. But this young woman was neither and it was a nuisance, it might even be dangerous. Even so they could not stop now, she refused even to think of that Miss Pentecost told herself sharply; if they were to save Isola San Giorgio, if she herself was ever to get away from it, they had to go on. They had to find some means of dealing with Simone, or persuading her to see it their way, when the time came.

Mrs Teestock appeared in the sitting-room again, came out on to the patio, a sudden bulky silhouette, and called softly, 'Emilia; are you there?' For a moment Emilia Pentecost felt a flare of unreasoning irritation against the never ending kindliness, the eternal preoccupation with these damned islands and their people, but then she checked herself sharply. That was unkind; Aunt Judith Teestock had given her everything with unhesitating generosity, and would continue to give so long as she needed it; and so long as it was there to give. She said, 'Here, darling.'

Coming across the grass quickly Mrs Teestock peered at Emilia in the dim wavering light reflected from the water and started abruptly, 'Emilia, we must give this up. Miss Greenwood just won't do.'

'But why?' Emilia asked. 'Don't you like her?'

'I think she's quite charming. But she's very, very intelligent. And she's suspicious already.'

'You're worried,' Emilia Pentecost said gently. 'Now we've really started. Like stage fright. That's all.'

'It's more than that. Don't you see?' the older woman demanded. 'Don't you see how fatally easy it is to start something and then lose control of it? I'm afraid suddenly, Emilia. Five minutes ago I very nearly told that girl to go back to London.'

'No!' Emilia's voice was unnecessarily sharp and she added, 'I'm sorry, Judith. But we've always agreed that we'd wait to see how it worked out.'

Mrs Teestock did not answer and Emilia thought that she had been wise not to tell her that d'Espinal was in Venice already, clearly for his own reasons; that would have frightened her still more; it was obvious already that there were going to be things which one would have to keep from Judith. She went on, 'Becky would want to know why. After all she started it; she insisted on our getting Simone in the first place. She'd never forgive you, and the girl would be very angry, she'd have a right to be;

and even more suspicious. You must see that.'

'I suppose so.' But Mrs Teestock was still uneasy and she said, 'Very well. Let her decipher those notes if she wants to, and if she can; and that's all.'

'That's all we want for the present,' Emilia answered gently. 'It's the only thing to do. Leave everything as it is and wait to see what happens. That's so simple, darling; and we've plenty of time to decide.'

Mrs Teestock was now looking across at the lights of Venice almost as if she could see something threatening there. She said, 'I'm getting nervous of you, Emilia; that's the truth. You've been so inflexible lately. You imagine you can manage everybody; but you can't, you know.' She laughed uncertainly. 'You don't have enough to interest you here. We ought to find you a husband; that's what you really need. And we could do with a man about San Giorgio.'

'A rich one, I hope, if we're to keep this place up.' Emilia laughed too. 'I'm afraid we've left that a little late. I'm rather past my first youth don't you think? Let's go in, shall we? It's getting quite cold.'

CHAPTER THREE

D'Espinal emerged with Annunzietta from the candle-lit dimness of the church of San Trovaso into the bright early sunlight looking slightly pious. His immediate need now was coffee laced with cognac, and he gently steered the old lady and her market baskets into a café-bar on the corner of the square. In an atmosphere of steam and the scent of fresh bread, against a not unpleasant working clatter from the ancient boat yard across the canal, he listened benevolently to the shrill local gossip for a time before saying, 'Now, my 'Etta, you have it clear what we want? Every word, every whisper you can hear about the Ca' Vespucci and the people who live in it. While I shall repair to the Sant' Angelo steps to find Marco the grandson of Andreas; the gondolier.'

She chuckled appreciatively, her old shrewd eyes snapping with anticipation. 'You speak like an opera. You should be at the Fenice Theatre.'

It was a fair walk but d'Espinal was in no hurry. At the Accademia he leaned on the parapet of the vast bridge, surveying the sparkling bustle of the Grand Canal, before going on to the other bank, passing into the grey Campo of San Stefano and then plunging into a maze of narrow streets and backwaters to come out finally on the spectacle of the Canal again. There were half a dozen gondolas rocking at the steps, where he enquired, 'Marco Battista, if you please?' and a dark stocky young man with a flash of gleaming teeth under the straw hat of his trade answered, 'Pronto, signore.' D'Espinal approved of him at once; he said, 'To the Ca' Vespucci on the Rio della Fava.'

Seated regally in the black leather armchair, he waited until they were swaying out into the canal and then announced, 'My old friend, your grandfather Andreas, sent me to you. He tells me that you know the lagoon very well.'

'Also most of the gondoliers and boatmen,' Marco said modestly. 'How is the ancient one?'

'He still enjoys his wine and complains that you have not been to take a glass with him these several weeks. You should see to it. Does your knowledge extend to the Isola San Giorgio Piccolo?'

'That one to the west of San Erasmo, in the direction of San Francesco del Deserta? It is very small and alone; with a villa on it, and the padrona is wealthy; fabulously wealthy, yet saintly nevertheless. They say she is a good friend to the people who live on the islands out there.'

'Saintly...' d'Espinal repeated. He considered that for a few minutes and then asked, 'Is that all you can tell me? I would like to know more; in particular about the people on San Giorgio. More especially about a young signorina who arrived yesterday. Who she is and, if possible, what she is here for.'

Behind him Marco whistled softly. He said, 'That rings with something, signore. In one minute now we shall be in quieter water, and I will tell you.' They swayed to the right and passed under the sudden shadow of a bridge into a silent canal between high blank walls; it was chilly and dark green but quiet, and Marco went on, 'There is another person in Venice asking much the same questions. Not concerning the young signorina, of whom I have not heard anything as yet, but about the other ladies on the island.'

'What?' D'Espinal screwed round to look up at him. 'Who is that?'

'His name is Giacomo Vespe or something like it, and he is at the house of one, Manetti, on the Via Garibaldi. I heard of this because the word has been put around about him,' Marco explained. 'He is a bad client. It seems that he hired Toni Piero to take him out to San Giorgio Piccolo, and he asked things like you have. When they arrived there he had Toni cruise close in, wanting to know this and that, more than Toni could tell him. But on coming back to Venice he refused to pay Toni's just and proper charge. There was some discussion, but then one of the Municipal Guards appeared and Vespe paid at once and hurried off.' Marco added virtuously, 'For my part I say that any man who asks such questions and then runs away from a Municipal Guard must have something on his mind; something not very good.'

'So,' d'Espinal breathed. 'And does your warning of a bad client run to his description?'

'Yes indeed. He is past middle age, and has a hard, angry face. He wears expensive clothes, but badly; not as you do, signore. And jewellery; a pin in his tie, and rings. Also he has only the thumb and the first and second fingers on his left hand. Toni, who says he is a desperado, thinks it could be the last two have been shot away some time.'

D'Espinal nodded slowly. 'You give me the picture. It seems to me, young man, that everything your old grandfather says of you is quite correct. I shall tell him so. And now, if you please, the Ca' Vespucci.'

It was in a shadowy green siding off the Rio Fava, where the only movement was a wavering pattern of ripples reflected up on to ancient red brick walls and grey stone. In its way, d'Espinal thought, the house itself although somewhat gloomy was still not without beauty. A pair of newly painted blue and white mooring posts, landing steps, and a heavily studded timber water gate. The ground floor openings were barred with wrought iron grilles in front of cloudy green glass, and above them was a carved and fretted balcony supporting a line of arches on slender, spiralled pillars. Over these again was a row of tall, deep windows with decorated lintels and finally, under the wide eaves, another row of smaller ones.

He found it difficult to date. It looked as if until the last few years it had been carefully kept in good condition and even restored in places; but the base was certainly very old and the coat of arms carved above the entrance was almost obliterated. The quarterings were gone, although the crest was clear enough, and one d'Espinal did not remember ever having seen before; a skull wearing a coronet. Curious and rather grim, he thought. 'They say it is an unlucky house,' Marco murmured. 'And that the old woman who lives here is a strange one and she keeps fabulous treasures inside.'

D'Espinal caught a faint note of speculation in his voice. He was obviously a quick witted young man, and it was quite possible that he might connect an interest in this house with its treasures. And why 'treasures', d'Espinal wondered; why not simply 'a fabulous picture'? Reflecting that whispers might pass both ways along the canals of Venice he said, 'This is an affair of your ancient grandfather, the Padrone Raffaele and myself. It is, as it were, an interest of the family and you will keep it a close secret; even from your friends. And now if you care to take me so far we will go to drink that glass of wine with old Andreas.'

The sunlight caught on Simone's tawny blonde hair and white dress as they all waited at the landing steps on Isola San Giorgio; Mrs Teestock wearing brownish grey tweeds, Miss Pentecost a restrained white blouse and black skirt, and Pietro standing by as sidesman in his uniform jacket and trousers. It was a beautiful opalescent midday, the lagoon rippling gently in patterns of turquoise and green, Venice shimmering in distant gold through the haze, and a big white and silver launch cutting in towards the island on wide wings of spray. Watching it approach Simone wondered rather wildly how you addressed a princess in Venice; even if her christian name was Becky.

The launch swung round and its motors coughed and died. There were three men aboard, all wearing something like a sort of private naval uniform and white yachting caps, and as it edged up and bumped gently two of them stepped out carrying a small mat which they laid down on the wet bricks, while the steersman turned to assist the person who appeared from the curtained midships cabin. Then as the first two steadied the boat he handed her tenderly up from the deck, while Pietro stepped forward smartly to hold out his forearm for her to rest on, and she stood for a moment blinking in the sunshine; a most surprising princess.

She was a small, plump old lady with a red face and a button of a nose, carefully waved grey hair, faded but still quick and shrewd blue eyes, and expensive yet somehow oddly unbecoming black clothes. She seemed to be insignificant and drab against the bright garden and blue sea and sky, and she peered at them uncertainly before Mrs Teestock said, 'Dear Becky, it's so nice to see you.'

'You couldn't keep me away,' the princess answered briefly, looking past them at Simone, peering again with her eyes slightly screwed up. She asked, 'Is that her?' and Mrs Teestock started, 'May I present...' but she interrupted, 'You don't need to make a performance of it.' In a rich Yorkshire accent she said, 'Eh, love, it's that good of you. To come all this way for an old woman like me.'

Simone was half aware of Miss Pentecost studying them both with a sort of clinical detachment, as if watching something she herself had planned start to work itself out, but at that moment she was more conscious of the princess's transparent pleasure. It was infectious and she smiled rather warily at first but then laughed, held out her hands like seeing an old friend again after a long time and answered, 'I've been waiting to meet you too.'

'Well now that's settled,' Mrs Teestock said. Again there seemed to be an odd note of uncertainty in her voice, and a little over briskly she added, 'One can see already, it's going to be a great success.'

They all turned across the grass towards the low pink house with its vine pagola and patio, with the sky and lagoon each reflecting the other like blue mirrors.

Simone did not like the look of the Ca' Vespucci; she understood now the repeated careful hint this morning that she might find it somewhat gloomy. It was still only mid afternoon when the launch crept in but the canal was already dark green and shadowy although the sun, striking across the eaves of the old red brick building opposite, still picked out the twisted columns and arches above. Neither did she much care for the thin, sad butler who met them in the hall, with its uneven floor, bare walls and eroded marble staircase; and when the princess asked, 'Any callers, Luciano?' he answered in English, 'No callers, madame.' It sounded like a ritual question always asked and always answered the same.

But there was a second and heavily carpeted hall at the head of the stairs, with a maid waiting there. She was a few years older than Simone herself, brisk and sharp; a neat figure already slightly plump, bronze hair and full red lips, snapping black eyes now veiled with professional restraint. They rested on Simone for a moment, almost conspiratorially, while the princess announced, 'This is Maria. And I'll thank you,' she told her, 'to look after Miss Greenwood the same as you do me.' Maria murmured, 'It will be a privilege, madame,' and once again her eyes seemed to convey some kind of amused partnership. The princess announced, 'Miss Greenwood can do with some tea.'

The butler led them past a pair of doors open to a

glimpse of what looked like an ornate reception room, and into a wide corridor where there were high-backed chairs placed stiffly against the walls; at the end a leaded window with dim green glass, and under it a carved and painted bride chest. Half way along they turned left under an archway, climbing a flight of stairs again to a second passage; a little less like a museum than the other below. Here the arches were hung with tapestry drapes, and the doors now were in modern polished mahogany. Puffing slightly the princess said, 'It's a regular rabbit warren this place.'

Luciano opened the last door and stood aside. It was a small, crowded and surprising room; almost as surprising as the princess herself, Simone thought, not unlike an antique store where the contents are displayed without thought of period or value. A clutter of personal oddments and faded photographs, a matching pair of Highland pictures after the style of Landseer; a battered roll top desk against a beautiful old faldstool, one fine Venetian lamp and two more with ruffled pink silk shades and a glittering modern Milanese cocktail cabinet. On the right were two more leaded windows, but this time in clear glass protected with bars outside, and opposite these a door into a second room.

Only one wall was left bare; that facing the entrance from the corridor. It was soft, neutral grey and against all the rest its simplicity was almost shockingly austere; it seemed to be somehow half religious. Exactly in the centre was a shallow recess perhaps four feet wide; in this was a gallery strip light fixed above closed dark green velvet curtains and below stood a narrow rosewood table on which was lying only a tooled leather case, again in dark green.

The princess said, 'It's a bit of a rummage sale, this lot. Some of it's from the time we got married, before my Arthur made his money. He wouldn't have let me have it about when we got set up here, he turned a bit fancy in his taste. But when he died I felt I had to have some of the old things around me again. D'you think I'm a daft old woman?' she asked.

Simone studied her thoughtfully. She was already getting to know something about Becky; lonely and afraid of the bleak years ahead, perhaps in some ways even naïve; but not daft. She said, 'Far from it.'

'There's all too many round here who do.' For a moment Becky looked surprisingly spiteful and then asked, 'What d'you make of Judy Teestock and Emilia?'

'I really don't know,' Simone answered cautiously. 'I haven't known them long enough. Miss Pentecost seems a rather managing sort.'

The princess cackled. 'She rules the roost if you ask me. She had a sort of breakdown in Paris years back, a bad love affair with some no good artist, and Judy took her in. She's fond of Judy in her own way but she don't have two ha'pennies of her own to rub together and that's a niggling thing for a woman like Emilia Pentecost.'

'And I am not going to be bogged down with local gossip,' Simone told herself. She said, 'Tell me about Mr Vespucci.'

Becky considered her quizzically. 'You know how to shut people up; and you stick to business. There's good blood in you, girl; and it shows. My Arthur would've taken to you. He could see quality when he met it. Like when he found this...'

There was a white cord hanging beside the curtains in the alcove and Becky reached out to it; the drapes slid apart while the strip lamp above came on to reveal what hung behind. It was not large, no more than twenty-four by thirty inches, and it was set in a plain severe frame; but the picture itself was luminous with rich soft colour. Restrained, yet somehow extraordinarily sensuous; idealized but still a living and appealing face, it was the portrait of a girl set against a pastoral background glowing with what d'Espinal would have called the light of a permanently golden afternoon in Tuscany.

Simone stared at it without speaking; and the princess said, 'Simonetta Vespucci. Painted for Giullano de' Medici.'

It was a head and bust; there was a half smile, faintly enigmatic on the lips, a hint of question in the eyes, and a long twist of tawny blonde hair falling over the right shoulder. She wore only a heavy gold and emerald necklace, gleaming against the pale skin and supporting what appeared to be an enamelled pendant between the small breasts.

'I don't know what to say,' Simone murmured, and then asked, 'It is by Botticelli?'

'My Arthur reckoned so. And that's good enough for me. Arthur reckoned it was the most realistic he ever painted. Medici ordered it that way.' There was a strange expression on Becky's face. She peered at the picture, again with her eyes screwed up. 'To tell the truth I can't see it all that well; not without my spectacles. But I know what to say all right.

There's a curse on it.'

Simone stared at her incredulously. She said, 'No, Becky, that really is daft.'

'D'you think so? Well it killed Arthur. Leastways he died of it. And he never told me in so many words, but I've got an idea he wasn't the first.'

'I see.' Simone tried deliberately to sound matter of fact and businesslike. 'And that's what you want me to find out?'

'I want you to find out where that picture came from. And other things.'

They were interrupted by a light tap on the door, and it was opened by Luciano with Maria behind him wheeling in a tea trolley. She smiled at Simone, again with that curious hint of partnership, and for a moment her eyes settled on the picture before dropping to the green leather case on the table beneath it. 'Madame,' she murmured, and Becky answered, 'We'll serve ourselves,' and then waited for the door to close behind the two of them again before saying, 'Maria's all right, but she takes too much on herself. You'll want to watch that. Give her an inch and she'll help herself to a mile.'

'We were talking about the picture,' Simone suggested gently. 'And Mr Vespucci.'

'In a minute, love.' Becky eyed the trolley doubtfully. 'I don't drink all that much tea.' She glanced sideways and asked, 'D'you mind if I have a drop of something else?'

'Becky, please,' Simone protested, 'why should I?'

'You never know,' the old lady muttered. 'Young people often get so disapproving.' From somewhere in the roll top desk she produced a pair of spectacles saying, 'I hate these things but I can't see without 'em,' and turned to the cocktail cabinet; Simone heard the chink of a bottle and Becky went on defensively, 'You might as well hear it from me, if I don't tell you somebody else will. I'm inclined to take a drop too much, and I know it.' With her back to Simone she added suddenly, 'I don't want to put you off.'

She came back with the glass in her hand and went on, 'It's like this. You could stay over there, on the island, but I should like you to stop here. I'll be straight, love, apart from doing Arthur's papers for me I want your company. This house needs a bit of young life about; and so do I.' Simone started to say something but Becky went on, 'Just let me finish. I've had a little suite put ready for you; a bedroom and a bath and a private sitting-room; Maria's a good lady's maid so long as you keep her in her place, and there's the boat always ready for when you feel like a trip anywhere.' She watched Simone carefully. 'Come to that, I thought we might go out a bit together; have a nice meal now and again or run over to the Lido. Or the theatre. The Fenice's a pretty little theatre; and I haven't been there for years.'

'It sounds wonderful,' Simone said. 'But I thought I was coming here to work.'

The princess chuckled. 'You get prim sometimes, love.' She added, 'I just don't want you to think I've been taking things for granted.'

'But why should I?'

Becky seemed to be slightly uneasy. 'I'm going to give a big party; but there's plenty of time for that. You wanted to know about Arthur.' She put the glass down, went back to the desk and returned carrying a silver-framed photograph. 'My Arthur was a great man.' And she was still in love with him, Simone thought. 'As different as chalk and cheese from that other little crook; I married him for the company. I'll tell you about Stefan some other time, when we want a good laugh.'

It was a plump, middle aged man, slightly balding, with an aggressive and acquisitive mouth, an obstinate chin and a strong patrician nose. A contradictory face; the face of a man who would stop at nothing to get what he wanted, yet with a surprising touch of romanticism about the eyes. In fact, Simone thought, it was a Renaissance face; you could see, not the same features perhaps, but something of the same character looking out at you from any number of portraits from Florence or Venice of the fifteenth century.

Becky said, 'He was in a class by himself. When he was fourteen his mother was a widow, she was running one little cook shop in Sheffield; you know, hot pies and faggots and the like. They used to be a big thing in that part of the world. His father was a stone carver who came from Italy to make his fortune. He never did, poor man, but Arturo more than put that right. By the time he was twenty they'd got a chain of shops. That was when I met him.' She paused but Simone did not dare to interrupt, and it was very quiet in the little room until Becky went on again. 'He was handling his first million at thirty-five; by the time he was fifty he said he'd got all he was ever likely to need, and we sold up and came out here where he'd always wanted to be. That was when he took up the family history.' She turned to look at the portrait, now with her spectacles on, and then glanced back at Simone.

'He really thought he was one of the Vespucci?'

'He reckoned he might be, but was too level headed to count on it. It was just the name; and the history. He'd been studying it for years, back in England. And he'd never stopped being an Italian. He got the language from his father and he kept that up; and taught himself French and German into the bargain...'

'He must have been a wonderful person.'

'He was determined. That was why he never gave up however much the others treated him like a crackpot; the real professors and experts and such. They said he'd got a bee in his bonnet and it made him right wicked. There was only one who didn't. Old Rutilio Lenardi at the Accademia. He and Arthur were as thick as thieves.' She chuckled. 'I remember Lenardi once saying to me "What a pity Arturo did not devote himself to scholarship instead of wasting his time making all those millions".'

Young and excited Simone said, 'But Becky, that's wonderful! I must meet him.'

Becky shook her head. 'He's dead, love. Before Arthur found that lot.' She nodded at the portrait. 'The year before.'

'Oh dear,' Simone murmured. 'That's unfortunate.'

'It is that,' the old woman answered, slightly amused.

'And you've no idea where Mr Arturo found the picture?'

'Somewhere about Florence. It must be in the notes. All I know for sure, when he came back with it, is that he telephoned me from Forli. He said he was on the way home and he'd arrive late that night.

I was to see the staff were all in bed and sit up to let him in myself. That was November, nineteen sixty-two.'

'But what did he tell you?'

'Nothing, love; nothing at all. A twelve-month or so before he did say he was in the way of something bigger than just a book about the Vespucci, but the less it was talked about the better; and when Arthur got tight mouthed it was no use asking questions. Not even the night he came home. It was one o'clock in the morning and he was sick and exhausted. He just opened that picture up, and the other things, and I thought they were beautiful; I didn't know what they were going to do for us then. And he said, "Listen Becky; I got 'em honest, as honest as they could be got. That's all I'm going to say until I've cleared it all up and they go back where they belong."'

'"Back where they belong,"' Simone repeated. 'And you've no idea?'

'Not from that day to this. It's what I want you to find out.'

'If I can. And then?'

'That's all, love. Arthur only had three months left. He got that wall rebuilt; and other things arranged. I'll show you in a minute. And then he was taken off with pneumonia, in the February. We always used to go away to somewhere warm in the winter; but that year we didn't. He swore he'd never leave the house while Simonetta was in it.' She looked past Simone at the picture and then added, 'It's a long time ago now. You get over things.'

'"Never leave the house,"' Simone said. 'Was he worried about something?'

'I thought he was on the look out right up to the end. And the last night he whispered "There's only two fingers on his left hand".' She stopped and then went on, 'He could've been trying to tell me something but he never got it out; he was too far gone. But later on he just about managed to say "God grant her peace".' Becky's voice was carefully unemotional. 'It was that gave me the idea he might not have been the only one to die of Simonetta Vespucci.'

'He could have been speaking of Simonetta herself,' Simone said. She asked, 'Have you ever seen anyone with only two fingers on his left hand?'

'Not then nor ever since. Eh,' Becky added. 'Listen to me telling an old woman's hard luck tale. And there's something more I want to show you.' She got up briskly and went back to the picture, to the green leather case under it. 'Come and look, love.'

She lifted the lid; and immediately the soft light glowing down from the portrait seemed to blaze into a sudden flare of green fire. Simone caught her breath sharply; for a second or two she stared down before looking up at the portrait again. It was the heavy necklace which Simonetta there was wearing, the same deep lambent glow of twelve huge cabuchon emeralds set in intricately worked gold and supporting the same enamelled pendant—a half heraldic device displaying a woman standing with flames at her feet against a background of the rising sun and a dark blue sky.

'It's the necklace Giuliano de' Medici gave her for the Great Tournament of Florence in 1475. That's the design he had on his banner, done by Botticelli again; so Arthur said. Simonetta Vespucci representing Pallas Athene as the Goddess of War, standing among burning olive branches.'

With the green reflecting in her eyes Simone looked at them. For the first time she felt a presentiment of evil and she said, 'To leave them here, Becky; open like this...'

The princess cackled; a shrewd old Yorkshire woman once more. 'Can't you see? It's too bright for genuine; it's a replica Arthur had made on the quiet. The real thing's here all right, in a safe behind the picture.' Her voice dropped. 'Along with something else. And, I'll tell you straight, it's something I don't much fancy; never have. Arthur reckoned it'd be the last thing that poor child had in her hands the minute she died.'

'What is it?'

'All in good time. It's best left where it is; and I can't show it you now even if I wanted to. The keys are at the bank; it's a right royal command performance to get that lot open.' She chuckled again. 'Poor Stevey used to give himself nightmares trying to work out how to do it, the little crook. But he never could. My Arthur tied it up too tight for him or anybody else. I'll show you, so you'll know. Just give the picture a little push, that's all.'

Simone reached out carefully, and as she touched only the picture frame there was an immediate strident shrilling of bells; in this room, somewhere deeper in the house and even outside above the canal. She flinched back automatically, rather angrily, and it stopped at once; the sudden quietness seemed to be almost as painful as the noise. 'I must say...' Simone started, but before she could finish the door was flung open to show two of the men from the boat standing there shoulder to shoulder, with Luciano craning nervously behind them. One of them asked sharply, 'Principessa?' and Becky answered, 'There's no trouble; I'm only checking.' She watched them go, waited for Luciano to leave and then asked, 'You see what I mean?'

Becky took up her drink again and went on, 'There now, love, I've said all there is to say; talking too much, as usual. You ought to know now what it means to me having you here. I don't mind telling you straight out that when I read the piece about you in that women's magazine and saw your photograph I couldn't rest. I thought it was a sign from Providence.'

'I wouldn't put it as high as that. It was a professional journalist building up a romantic story.'

Becky shook her head. 'The Lord works in mysterious ways, child; and He don't hurry Himself.' She looked at the portrait again and then back at Simone. 'There's a likeness, you know.'

'It's coincidence,' Simone insisted.

'Call it what you like, it suits me. And it would've suited Arthur. Away back years ago, when he used to talk about it, he always reckoned that Giuliano had a child by Simonetta. And it took the Vespucci name. You could well be a descendant, love. Heredity's a funny thing.'

'Not so funny as that. I'm sorry, Becky, it's pure speculation. I really can't allow it.'

The princess cackled once more. 'Little Miss Prim. So have it your own way. Now,' she went on, 'I'm going to send you back to San Giorgio or you'll be late for dinner. While you're on your way I'll telephone Judy Teestock to tell her that I'll have Maria come over to fetch your baggage and bring you back tomorrow morning.'

CHAPTER FOUR

With his hands behind his back d'Espinal was walking thoughtfully in Paolo Raffaele's arcade gallery and studying the collection; while the sinister cat Cesare Borgia, who seemed to have taken an inexplicable fancy to him, lay indolently in a bar of sunlight like a small gold and silver tiger. Paolo's pictures, the minor masters, always pleased d'Espinal. Giovanini Monti, the son of a beggar and Verdizzotti, a pupil of Titian, Padovanino who painted impossible history and Conti of Ancona who worked for Pope Gregory; the School of Siena, School of Urbino. Sometimes a little naïve, d'Espinal thought, sometimes so humanly clumsy, yet all good worthy people.

But today his appreciation was at best absent minded. Even the contemplation of a little Manetti after the style of Caravaggio—which he considered Paolo was pricing far too modestly—failed to please him. He was thinking more about a rumour, which Annunzietta had picked up, that the Princess Kodaly was planning soon to give an important party; and about a curious story, this time from the grandson of Andreas and his network of gondoliers, that the mysterious fellow with a mutilated left hand had called at the service entrance to the Ca' Vespucci late last night. Above all he was wondering how far the ladies of San Giorgio would be content to leave himself here in peace; if he read the character of the woman Pentecost correctly it would not be for long.

That was like speaking of the devil. He heard Andreas say, 'In the gallery, signorina,' and quick footsteps on the pavement; saw the cat Borgia stare haughtily back along the gallery with its tail twitching, and turned to find Miss Pentecost standing there. She said, 'How charming, Mr d'Espinal. What a delightful place.'

'It would please Raffaele to hear you say that,' he told her, and then asked, 'May I present Cesare Borgia?' She stared at him, and just as solemnly he added, 'We also have Messire Niccolo Machiavelli somewhere about the place.'

'I'm sure you must have. I'd like to meet him.'

'While I,' d'Espinal smiled heavily, 'am equally sure he could not tell you anything.'

'You're very kind, but shall we drop the nonsense? Why are you in Venice a week early?'

'Your tone displeases me, madame. I am visiting my friends and about my business. Now say, Miss Pentecost, how did you find me?'

Her eyes rested on him for a moment; not without appreciation, he thought complacently. 'You're noticeable. Most baggage porters work at their own stations, and I imagine you tip extravagantly. I went to the Air Terminal and asked.' She added, 'Your business is the sale of forged pictures.'

D'Espinal walked away for a few paces and stopped to gaze meditatively at a somewhat worried looking Madonna and a fat and singularly undivine Child. He asked, 'How do you know that? As I recollect you were strangely coy on the subject when we met in London. How do you know, Miss Pentecost?'

'Have you ever heard of Ponzi in Milan? The most efficient private detectives in the world. I simply asked them who were the most crooked art dealers in Europe. They gave me your friends in Paris; and you ...'

'I perceive I have greatness thrust upon me.'

'If you can call it that.'

'Do you question my morals?' he demanded. 'Tell me, if I can give some poor rich person a glimpse of the light by providing a thing of beauty, although perhaps not by the accepted artist, what harm is there?' He said virtuously, 'I have never sold a bad picture in my life. The very thought disgusts me ... What do these people buy, madame? A work of art, or a name?'

'In the case of Tina Drikos it was Correggio,' Miss Pentecost murmured reflectively. 'A study for one of the "Loves of Jove". For a nominal figure of fifty thousand pounds.' She came closer to d'Espinal. 'Do you know Mrs Messina-Silvestro; and Professor Venturi?'

'One has heard of them.'

'The Silvestro is an arrogant, meddling bitch. Venturi's an unpleasant little man. But an expert. And Silvestro almost owns him...' She stopped and it was very quiet in the gallery for a few seconds: Cesare Borgia scratched the back of his neck and then yawned rudely and stalked out into the garden. Miss Pentecost went on, 'Tina Drikos called in Venturi to assess the real value of her wonderful little study. Venturi told her that if one were generous it was perhaps two thousand lire.'

'Before God, madame,' d'Espinal exploded. 'That's

an insult. That sketch is a superb piece of work. You offend me.'

'I don't want to,' Miss Pentecost answered softly. 'Believe me. Let me finish; it's amusing. Venturi of course went cackling to Mrs Messina-Silvestro, and she naturally passed it on to Judith Teestock. And although Tina's spitting with fury she doesn't dare tell Aristide Drikos because that man really can be frightful on the slightest provocation. So she's now bribing Venturi to keep quiet; and we've all agreed to say nothing for the present.' She glanced at d'Espinal sideways. 'It's rather a delicate situation. You do see that?'

'One does indeed. Let us come to the nub of the matter. What exactly do you require of me?'

'I told you in London. Your professional expertise.'

'As I guess it,' d'Espinal said, 'you are engaged about some stratagem to filch or purloin a reputed Botticelli. I repeat; what part am I supposed to play?'

'Nobody's yet mentioned filching or purloining anything.'

'"I am but mad north-north-west; when the wind is southerly I know a hawk from a handsaw."'

She said, 'You will be asked to sell a Botticelli.'

'Let us sit down,' d'Espinal suggested. He led her to a marble seat at the far end of the gallery and sat brooding for a time, studying her from under his eyelids. She did not appear to be in the least put out by it and at last he announced, 'You are a very remarkable woman. Now...' Suddenly he dropped all his mannerisms; he became a businessman about a deal. 'Is it genuine?'

'I think there's no doubt of it.'

'You think? Is there an attestation? Provenance?'

'Attestation, no. Provenance...' She hesitated. 'There might be.'

'What does that mean?'

'We might find its history. We don't know yet.'

'Then what do you know?'

'About 1494,' Miss Pentecost said, 'Botticelli fell under the influence of Savonarola.'

'He joined the penitents; "The Weepers" they were called.' D'Espinal nodded gently. 'I am aware of it; and of that wicked friar's sermons. "What shall I say of you," he quoted, "ye painters who expose half naked figures to the public view." So?'

'Botticelli himself burned probably some of his finest works on the public bonfires. Others were destroyed later when the mobs sacked the Medici palace. This picture was saved.'

'One is tempted to ask how. It's a legend, madame. It means nothing. But let us grant it. So where has this masterpiece lain hidden all of these four hundred and eighty years?'

'Does that matter?'

'Don't you think so? Do you realize how much it might be worth?'

'I've heard a million pounds mentioned. I'd say more.'

'On the official market, given documentation and guarantees, X-ray analysis and all the rest, considerably more. But as I imagine you expect me to sell the work...' He paused dramatically. 'Precisely nothing; or at best any bargain I can make for it. One way the greatest art discovery in modern times; the other a mere slab of nicely arranged paint.'

'Of which you are an expert salesman.' Miss Pentecost smiled at him pleasantly. 'Mr d'Espinal, you have no choice. And of course you will retain a reasonable commission; which we fully expect to be considerable.'

D'Espinal brooded for a time before he answered. 'Very well. I will at least consider it. Let me have the details.'

'Not yet. They're rather complex. We shall tell you all you need to know at the right time.'

He started to speak, but then stopped suddenly and lowered his eyelids. With unusual docility he answered, 'As you wish. There is one thing, however. I must view this picture.'

'Is it essential?'

'Absolutely. I shall have plans to make; not the least being the small matter of getting it out of Italy. And there are certain contacts I must establish. It is even possible,' he went on dreamily, 'that some of my colleagues might join me in a small consortium, as it were, to purchase the thing ourselves. Yes,' he murmured, 'I like that. That way we could almost certainly offer you a far better price. But they'll ask at once, have I examined it?'

'I suppose so.' She looked down the gallery thoughtfully at two other people coming in at the far end with Paolo Raffaele. 'Very well, I'll arrange something.'

'As soon as possible. The negotiations may be very delicate; they will take time.'

'If I can.' She smiled at him again, and stood up gracefully.

'I think you must.' He opened the glass door out into the garden for her; they started slowly along the outside of the arcade towards the canal, and he went on, 'The other day at the air terminal you were meeting a young woman; it appeared also that you hurried her away with quite unseemly speed.'

'Did you speak to her?' Miss Pentecost asked quickly.

'I have my peccadilloes,' d'Espinal said piously, 'but even in an aircraft I am not in the habit of accosting ladies without a suitable introduction. I did not. What intrigued me, what still does, was a certain resemblance I perceived.' He waited, but Miss Pentecost did not say anything and he asked, 'Does she also have some part in this affair?'

'Your business is the picture; nothing else. You shouldn't be in Venice yet. I still don't understand why you are.'

'As a confederate,' he murmured sadly, 'I feel there is something less than perfect trust between us.'

'You amuse me; and you shouldn't.' She laughed rather breathlessly and sounded surprised. 'If you must be told this girl makes it all possible. She's ... Don't they call it a catalyst?'

'I see. Or do I? You appear to enjoy puzzles for their own sake, Miss Pentecost. How much does she know?'

Miss Pentecost stopped suddenly and half turned to face him. 'I'll tell you this. That girl's essential, but she could be difficult. If she is the whole thing might collapse. And if it does I shall tell Mrs Messina-Silvestro that I know who sold Tina Drikos that forged Correggio and where to find him.' She considered the well dressed, well fed figure, the air of easy luxury. 'She's inconceivably meddlesome, that woman, and it would cost you fifty thousand pounds;

or several years in prison. Greek millionaires can be horribly spiteful.'

'You make your point.'

'I'm sorry,' she said, 'I got a little melodramatic.' She moved on through the wrought iron gates to the footpath alongside the canal. 'But I mean it. Mr d'Espinal, for your own sake don't try to get in touch with that girl. If you do meet her, don't try to ask her any questions, don't tell her anything.'

For a moment d'Espinal thought curiously that Miss Pentecost looked almost appealing; he remarked, 'The whole affair becomes as crazy as Paolo Raffaele's cats.'

'It's been a long time working out.' She seemed to be speaking more to herself than to him. 'And nothing's going to stop it now.'

She moved on, but he said, 'One moment more, Miss Pentecost. I am a man of some considerable insight and even more observation. Allow me to tell you this. You are a beautiful woman; and I believe that the ferocity with which you are pursuing this business is doing you an injury. And perhaps others with you. Beware lest you fall into error...'

Miss Pentecost stared at him. Neither of them moved before she swung round abruptly and started away. D'Espinal watched her until she crossed the small iron bridge at the end of the canal, and then he turned back into Paolo's quiet garden. On the whole he felt not dissatisfied. He had a great deal to think about now; and a glass of wine in the pleasant shade of the balcony would not come amiss.

Miss Pentecost walked back through the narrow streets of the craftsmen's quarter, stopping to watch a stonemason at work and a cabinet maker in a sharp-scented atmosphere of wood and resin, pausing again at an antique shop. There was a Venetian mirror in the doorway, and she stared at it like a picture of herself which she had never seen before; as if that self-satisfied character in the garden somehow had the knack of making you look at yourself a different way. Again she moved off impatiently alongside a canal, through an arched passage with crumbling walls, and out into a courtyard where there was a café with bright awnings, box trees in tubs and tables set out in the shade. Ordering coffee she sat there for a time, curiously solitary; watching the pigeons, two children playing some silent absorbed game of their own on the sunlit pavement, a woman sitting in a doorway making lace, before she asked the waiter abruptly, 'You have a telephone?'

She dialled quickly and when Luciano's sad voice murmured, 'Ca' Vespucci,' she answered, 'Signorina Spoletti.' Then it seemed to be a long time before Maria came, and Miss Pentecost said quietly, 'There's one small thing...'

'What is it?' Maria demanded. 'Miss Greenwood has arrived. The principessa is now with her in her suite. I should be with them too.'

Although it was unlikely that anyone could overhear, Miss Pentecost picked her words deliberately. 'It's about Miss Greenwood, Maria. She might not tell you herself, but she does not like to be interrupted in her work. She will wish you to say she is not at home to telephone calls; nor to visitors. And who receives your letters?'

'Alberto. He then hands them to Luciano.'

'She will prefer you to take hers. She is most particular about that.'

'Yes?' Maria stopped and then asked, 'Is there something?'

'Nothing,' Miss Pentecost said. 'Nothing at all. Only that we must take care of her. And when she leaves the house there should be someone not too far away. The principessa never goes out unattended; Miss Greenwood should have the same attention.'

'I think I see,' Maria answered. 'Very well, I will arrange that. I must leave now.'

'What are they doing today?'

'They have lunch at the Taverna di Fenice. Then the signorina is to start her work. Tonight the principessa thinks they will go to the Lido.'

'We must see that they are both very happy, Maria; that nothing worries them. Shall we ourselves have tea together soon? At the café opposite the Colleoni Statue on the Campo of St John and St Paul. In a day or two, perhaps? I'll call you.' She hung up and went out into the small, quiet square again.

Arturo Vespucci's study was at the foot of a short flight of steps from a passage out of the main corridor on the first floor, beneath the princess's own apartments and Simone's rooms. It seemed to be deliberately remote, with two tall windows looking down on a green, deserted back-water canal; and, however much Arturo had chosen to fill the rest of his house with Florentine antiques, he had left his own corner of it as simple and bare as a scholar's cell. A big desk and high backed chair, a reading stand placed near the wide bookcase, and an incongruous steel filing cabinet like an afterthought. There were only four pictures on the austere white walls; three recognizably fifteenth-century Italian in their style and soft colouring, and one other which seemed to be oddly discordant—a rather overworked and modern painting of the Ponte Vecchio in Florence.

Simone looked around with a curious impression that the real owner of the room had only just left it, and the princess said, 'Nothing's been changed.' She glanced at Simone uneasily. 'I feel as if I've got a goose walking over my grave. I didn't sleep a lot last night, and kept thinking about that girl in the old story, the one somebody gave a beautiful box to and when she took the lid off to see what was inside she let all the trouble in the world out ... I'm talking daft again,' she added briskly, and held out a small key to Simone. 'Here love, you open the cabinet. Happen it'll be a bit stiff. I had to have a locksmith in and get a new key for it; the old ones took a walk.' Simone stared at her, and she explained, 'They got lost.'

There was a dry tone to her voice and Simone asked, 'You mean they were stolen? But when, Becky?'

'Long enough back; in Stevey's day. Don't look so dumbstruck, child. It don't matter much. Stefan Kodaly was a crook, but he hadn't got the brains of a weasel, and my Arthur always said that only him and God could read what was important in there.'

Rather dryly herself Simone said, 'That doesn't give me much chance then. But you never had the keys back?'

'I didn't bother. Stevey always turned as sulky as a child when you went on at him about anything. Anyway he got himself killed two or three months after, and that was the end of it.'

When it was opened there seemed to be nothing like Pandora's Box about the filing cabinet. The two bottom shelves were empty, the next held only three stiff covered quarto note books and a thin file, and the top contained six or eight bulky manilla folders. Not so much as Simone had expected, and after all she had heard about Arturo Vespucci so far she was vaguely disappointed. Laid out in rows and opened up on the desk they appeared simply untidy. Each one was filled with what looked like random scrap paper; loose sheets of foolscap, pages apparently torn from different note books, even an hotel menu card, and used envelopes cut open and flattened; some covered with writing and many more with only a few notes. About half, the first three folders, were written in contracted but still recognizable Italian while the remainder were in what appeared to be a curious angular script, and at first sight incomprehensible. The clear writing on the foolscap sheets was neat and precise; on the envelopes and odd scraps it was often a rough scrawl. Simone breathed, 'Well.'

The princess chuckled. 'That was Arthur all over. He couldn't bear to waste a bit of paper. I always thought it was because when he was a boy he had to buy his own and he knew the value of it.' She picked up one of the envelopes and turned it over. 'I sent him that. See? Hotel Arnolfo, Florence. When he was away he'd always telephone me where he was off to next, and I used to write to him pretty well every other day. Here's another; Albergo Benedetta, Genoa ... There's a lot of them.'

Becky was transparently pleased, like a child; but

Simone, staring at that envelope, was conscious of the first flush of excitement which comes when one has stumbled on to an open lead, just a line into the confusion however unimportant it might seem to be at first. She pushed her heavy glasses on, read off the postmark, 'Venice, June 23, 1959', and turned over and examined some of the others.

'Becky,' she said, 'that might be important. Because by checking the addresses against the post dates on all those envelopes we can trace exactly where he went; and when. And perhaps even what he was following up at that time.'

'Eh,' the old lady breathed. 'That's bright. After all these years.'

Simone nodded absently, considering the mass of papers, but still thinking of the lost key. 'Would you say they're still as Arthur left them?'

Becky seemed doubtful. 'So far as I know. Though I wouldn't be surprised if Stevey had a look at 'em once or twice. But I've told you, love, they'd be beyond him. Here,' she went on briskly, 'at least I can make myself useful. I'll do a list of all those envelopes for you.'

In fact Simone would have liked to be left alone then, but she murmured, 'That will be a help,' and turned to the manuscript books herself. Two of them were blank, but the third was filled to about half way through with neat script in Italian, and on the first page it was dated October 1959 and headed "Simonetta Vespucci; a Study of the Woman". It seemed pompous and slightly self conscious.

It started, "In setting about this work I realize an ambition which has been with me for most of my life; not only as having the honour to bear that name myself, but also out of a dream that I might perhaps count this fascinating woman as one of my own distant forbears. I know of course that after nearly half a thousand years this can only remain such a dream. Yet for myself I choose to imagine that it has given me the determination—and dare I say the love?—to write of this tragic girl, who for too few years claimed the hearts and the minds of all Florence in that city's most illustrious period, with an attempt to understand and perhaps unravel some of the mysteries which lie around her."

Simone muttered, 'I hope he doesn't keep on like this,' and Becky said, 'Eh?' looking up over her spectacles. Simone turned slightly pink and asked, 'Have you read this?'

Becky peered at it, looking a little guilty. 'His book? To tell you the truth, love, I'm not any too good with written Italian. And Arthur himself wasn't all that satisfied with it.'

The next paragraph started, "I have lately returned from a pilgrimage to her birthplace near Genoa, the ancient seat of the Cattaneo family..." and Simone riffled over a few pages rather impatiently. Another passage caught her eye, perhaps because it was lightly marked in pencil down the margin as if Arturo had intended to refer back to it. "To confirm my own question, as to whether the love affair with Giuliano de' Medici was truly as platonic as it has always been supposed, Guiseppe Portigliotte writing of the consumptive type but still with reference to Simonetta says, 'There is a tendency to indulge in day dreams, an emotional liability ... and an exacerbation of the sexual instinct, though this is often given a Platonic colouring, as though to sublimate its material nature...' " That was interesting, she thought, but speculation.

She could read this at any time, and she flipped on to the end. But there a single name caught her attention again, Rutilio Lenardi who Becky had mentioned yesterday, and she read on automatically. "Nor am I alone in asking this. My old friend, Signor Rutilio Lenardi of the Accademia Library, Venice, has discussed this problem with me many times and indeed I cannot forget one such occasion when that very learned gentleman said, 'Poor child; poor lonely child after all that adulation'."

"But why this loneliness?" Arturo asked. "When she died aged only twenty-three, on April 27th 1476, so far as we can know none of those people who should have been closest to her were present. Yet it was known she was sinking, it had been known since April 18th; full time enough for any of them to arrive. Several days before the end Piero Vespucci, not Marco her husband but her father-in-law, had written to Lorenzo de' Medici (who had sent his own physicians) 'This night Maestro Stephano and Maestro Moyse debated whether to give her a medicine, which they concluded ought to be given, and so they gave it to her. It is not yet possible to see what effect it will have; God grant it may do what we desire.' It appears that except for Piero Vespucci, she died alone; neither her husband, her mother, nor her lover Giuliano de' Medici, was at the bedside. If this is true we must ask why were they not present?"

Simone frowned at that. It was interesting though again speculative, and it reminded her of Miss Pentecost; Miss Pentecost in her own office in London saying, 'He thought there might be something rather peculiar about Simonetta's death'. But how did she know? Simone wondered; those few lines seemed to be a hint of something which had never been suggested anywhere before. She asked suddenly, 'Becky, has Miss Pentecost ever read this?'

Becky was now completely absorbed with the notes and she answered, 'Eh?' peering at the book. 'Emilia Pentecost? She can't have done; it's never been out of this house. Why?'

It was odd, Simone thought. Miss Pentecost herself had told her that she only came to Venice about five years ago and Arturo had died in 1963 so she could not have got it from him. But it was not particularly important, only something else which seemed a little strange, and she said, 'It doesn't matter,' and turned back to the book. Arturo had finished there, half way down page thirty, and she put it aside to take up the last file. This contained only a disappointingly few letters. One headed The Städelsches Kunstinstitut, Frankfurt-am-Main, in German and referring to a supposed portrait of Simonetta by Sandro Botticelli and detailing its known history, two more from the Musée Condé at Chantilly; the first again about another picture of her by Piero di Cosimo, and the second announcing brusquely that the writer was not in a position to discuss the value of The Book of Hours of the Duc de Berry in that museum and he would not attempt to do so. That was dated December 1962 and Simone asked herself 'Why the Book of Hours of the Duc de Berry?' before she turned it over.

The next was again dated December of that year, headed Munich and once more in German, but this time written in a clear feminine hand. Clipped to it was a flimsy half sheet of paper obviously many years older than the letter itself; creased and dirty, covered with a half obliterated pencil scrawl and, so far as Simone could see, in Italian. Whatever that was, she thought, it would take time to decipher and she started on the letter.

This was easy. Roughly translated it read, "My dear Herr Vespucci; No, of course you do not distress me speaking of my husband. It is so long ago now and indeed, with the generous things you say of him, one feels grateful for your letter. I shall myself write to our old friend Signor Neri in Florence to thank him for giving you my address. But I fear there is very little I can tell you. Only that Paul was reported as missing, supposed killed in action. For a long time one prayed that he might return, but now perhaps the greatest grief is not knowing where he lies; except of course that it must be in Italy, which I know would comfort him. He loved Italy and it was always one of his sayings that there is something of the best of Italy in all of us.

"Of course I shall be most pleased and proud if you put him in the book you speak of, as I know he would be himself, and when you want it I will gladly give you all the information I can about him personally. As you say he had a sincere devotion to art although he realized that he was not a very good artist himself; painting for him was a pleasure of the vacations. Nevertheless you are so kind about him that I think you will perhaps like to have one of his pictures for Christmas, and this I am sending by a separate package. Please accept it with all of my good wishes. Yours very sincerely, Gertrud Meisner."

Simone was conscious again of her faint prickling of excitement. She asked, 'Becky; what do you know about a man named Paul Meisner?'

The princess blinked up at her and appeared to make an effort to come back into the present. 'Not a lot,' she answered at last, 'except he painted that picture,' nodding at the view of the Ponte Vecchio. Simone went across quickly to look at it, the signature and the date, 1937, and Becky added, 'The only thing is that Arthur said he wasn't much of an artist but he was a great man; and a brave man. That's about all he did say. I told you; he was right close mouthed all that time.'

'There's a letter here from Gertrud Meisner. Did anyone ever write to her again?'

'Arthur would've done. I never did.'

'Somebody's got to now,' Simone said crisply. 'I hope she's still there; it's been a long time. I'll make a note to do that in the morning.' She came back to the desk to take up the letter again. 'You know ... It's beginning to look as if nearly everybody connected with Simonetta's portrait is dead.'

Becky said, 'Yes,' watching the girl, thinking she looked young and vulnerable in spite of her cleverness, her big glasses and her sometimes comically severe manner. 'What did I tell you? I don't know,' she added slowly, 'but what we ought to let 'em rest in peace. I was thinking last night where this lot got my Arthur in the end, wondering whether it might do any more harm.'

Before Simone could answer there was a tap on the door and Maria appeared, matter of fact and over officious. 'Madame did not take her rest this afternoon,' she started.

'I still don't need a nurse; not yet,' the princess snapped back. 'You go and find us a cup of tea.' When the door closed she glanced sideways rather guiltily at Simone. 'I have to speak a bit sharp sometimes, Maria takes too much on herself.' Then she asked suddenly, 'Has she said anything about my party yet? It's not her place to, but she might.'

The change of subject was surprising, and Simone must have looked puzzled, for Becky went on, 'It'll be the first in this house for a long time, and I want you to have a big place in it.' For some reason she looked slightly uneasy and said, 'Perhaps it's taking too much for granted, but I never met the pretty girl yet who didn't fancy a party.'

'I am here to work, you know,' Simone reminded her.

Becky chuckled. 'Bless us, child, you look that serious. You're here for a bit of fun as well. Here, let's lock this stuff up again for now. We'll have that lazy lot get the boat out and run us over to the Lido for a breath of air and a walk down the Viale Elizabetta.'

CHAPTER FIVE

Judith Teestock was worried. Working on the exquisite golden embroidery of a new altar cloth for one of the island churches, she found she could not concentrate, and she had made several false stitches this morning leaving ugly marks on the white satin. Some of the girls would be sure to notice them when they came for their sewing class that afternoon, they had dreadfully sharp eyes; and already Graziella and Mrs Pietro had asked her if she was feeling unwell.

An hour ago she had tried to telephone Miss Greenwood at the Ca' Vespucci; she was not happy about her staying there and it had seemed the least she could do, to ask if all was well. But Maria had said that Signorina Greenwood was out; and no, the principessa had not risen yet. It was little enough perhaps yet it had seemed to suggest a new secrecy, something from which she was being deliberately excluded.

There was no doubt that Emilia had taken over. What had started as a dream, a fascinating puzzle in working out how it could be done had become an obsession; and Emilia, from being the intelligent, pleasant companion only too thankful for the peace and shelter of the island after her humiliating experience with that man those years ago was now a different person. She herself was partly to blame,

Mrs Teestock admitted dispassionately. She should have known from the beginning that a character like Emilia's would not tolerate the feeling of being a dependent indefinitely, however graciously the dependence was disguised; she should have known that Emilia was still young enough to want a life of her own and to have ambitions of her own. As stealing this picture and the other things was now a sort of perverted ambition.

And she was equally responsible for that. It was she who had first said 'If only it were possible ...' She had thought for years, she still thought, that she could do far more good with the Vespucci relics than Becky Kodaly would ever dream of doing. She could save San Giorgio with them, could give so much help in the islands, and in the end nobody would be any the worse off; certainly not Becky who was chained to Venice when she really ought to leave, who was drinking more every month because she was so unhappy here, and who really hated and was afraid of those things in any case. In the light of the ultimate good it was still quite justifiable. But only if it could be done without hurt to anyone—except perhaps a little passing distress for Becky, which would be more than compensated for by the freedom she would gain. That was what she must make quite clear to Emilia; the one absolute condition, that there must be no harm to anyone.

Emilia appeared then, carrying a silver tray with their morning coffee, sliding it on to the table under the window, and then coming to look at Mrs Teestock's work. 'How's it working out?' she asked.

'I'm making mistakes,' Mrs Teestock admitted. 'Because I'm worried. I've been thinking, Emilia; and

I'm still very undecided.'

Miss Pentecost stood with her finger tips resting on the altar cloth, apparently studying the intricate and beautiful design Mrs Teestock was creating, until the sound of Pietro's hoe at work out in the garden came in through the open window; then she moved across suddenly and closed it with a sharp little crack. 'About what?' she asked.

'Darling, don't be obtuse.' There was a trace of irritation in the older woman's voice.

'Are we back to the other night?'

'Going on from it. I'm worried about that girl. I tried to telephone her and Maria said she was out.'

'But why shouldn't she be?'

'No reason at all I suppose. Only it gave me a most unpleasant impression; as if she was being deliberately isolated.'

Miss Pentecost started to pour out the coffee with her back to Mrs Teestock; she asked carefully, 'Darling, isn't that really rather silly?'

'Perhaps it is. But we've never really worked out what to do about the girl. We've been too confident.' Miss Pentecost started to say something again but stopped and Mrs Teestock went on, 'From the moment Becky came across that ridiculous magazine article we assumed that she was a silly, shallow little creature. We assumed that if she was prepared to publish an obviously untrue story about being a descendant of Simonetta Vespucci she would be prepared to do almost anything else.'

'It was quite reasonable. Drink your coffee, Judith. You'll be getting one of your headaches.'

'We thought that because we wanted to think it. Now we know it's not true. She's got a streak of quiet determination; she'll never run away and leave Becky alone. Listen, Emilia; you're so obstinate. The whole plan depends on the fact that everyone in Venice is rather scornful of poor Becky, and nobody believes there is or ever has been a real picture or a real necklace...'

'It was your idea. You should know.'

'I wish I'd never thought of it. Because this girl will swear there's been a substitution, and whatever people might think of Becky some of them will believe her.'

'Even in the face of Mrs Medina-Silvestro and Professor Venturi?'

Mrs Teestock hesitated, thinking about that, and Emilia followed up her advantage quickly. 'I promise you, Judith, that the day after Becky's reception she'll be flying back to London. After that so far as anybody ever mentions her she'll simply be another one who fastened herself on to a gullible old woman for the sake of what she could get out of her. Like Stefan Kodaly. It's all so easy.'

'It's not easy; and it could get out of hand. Don't you see that?'

'Judith,' Emilia said, 'nothing ever gets out of hand unless one allows it to. You're worrying too much. I quite agree Miss Greenwood's not the type we wanted, but she'll never be able to prove anything and she's intelligent enough to see that. We shall have plenty of time to persuade her after Becky's party.'

Mrs Teestock stared at her. She whispered, 'What d'you have in your mind? You're changing every day; you're becoming evil.' Her voice rose sharply. 'You must understand me, Emilia; we shall not go through with this if it means the slightest harm to anyone.'

Miss Pentecost's own eyes widened. 'What d'you imagine I'm suggesting? Really, Judith,' she said sharply, 'it seems to me you've got some very peculiar ideas yourself.' She stopped and came over to the work table. 'I'm sorry, my dear. We're both a little hysterical.' Looking down at Mrs Teestock's embroidery she said softly, 'This really is beautiful.'

'I'm sorry too,' Mrs Teestock murmured. 'Mostly for your sake. I often think that in all these years here life's been slipping past you.'

'Life has a habit of slipping past.' Miss Pentecost turned away again. 'I must go and help Mrs Pietro, she's in one of her busy fits this morning.' She added, 'If it worries you so much, Judith, of course we can't go on. Only you should consider yourself; and all the work you do here. We both know it won't last much longer. Against the cost of everything your income goes down every quarter. You're going to find it quite terrible if you have to sell San Giorgio; and so are a lot of other people. I'm not so Christian as you; I wish I could be. But when I think of that old woman over there with so much; frightened of those things and wasting her life guarding them...'

'Please,' Mrs Teestock wailed suddenly. 'D'you think I haven't lain awake night after night thinking about it all. I don't know what to do.'

'Only you can decide,' Miss Pentecost told her gently. 'And there's still plenty of time to make up your mind.'

'What about that man?' Judith demanded. 'Mr d'Espinal? When does he arrive in Venice?'

'My dear, I'd almost forgotten him.' Miss Pentecost picked up the coffee tray and moved to the door. 'You don't need to be alarmed about Mr Harcourt d'Espinal; he's just a fat poseur. But really rather amusing. I think at least you ought to meet him. He's quite an experience. Now just think of all the good you can do, Judith,' she added. 'And don't forget your sewing class this afternoon.'

Out in the gracious vaulted corridor with its black and white tiled floor, ivory walls and a few small pictures, she waited for a few seconds biting her underlip and listening. She half expected Mrs Teestock to come out after her, but there was no sound from the sewing room and she turned away down two shallow steps into the hall. It was quiet and cool; somewhere in the house Graziella was singing about her work, and through the open double doors the garden was still glittering from a heavy rain shower during the night, but the lagoon was settling down into a sheet of soft placid blue once more. Miss Pentecost put down the tray, went across to the telephone and dialled quickly.

She heard it purring at the other end, then Luciano's voice, and she asked softly, 'Signorina Spoletti?' After a time Maria came on, and still watching the sewing-room door Miss Pentecost said, 'Maria, I think it would be nice to have tea together; I've a lot to tell you. Can you manage that this afternoon? On the Campo of St John and St Paul.'

D'Espinal walked slowly down the Via Garibaldi, approaching the old naval base and the dockyards, where you could see the masts and superstructures of cargo ships and liners towering over the buildings. It was a working quarter, busy and noisy on this hot brilliant morning, and full of the family affairs, the gossip and dark, bright children of any other small Italian town; the stalls and bars were for the people who lived here, the colour of fruiterers and grocers, a talkative barber's saloon, and newsvendors' stands packed with lurid journals.

He saw no particular purpose in this excursion except that he was becoming increasingly restless in the green peacefulness of Paolo's garden; an uneasy sense of events shaping in the background while he himself remained merely a pawn, as it were, waiting passively to be moved. It was a sensation which did not please him. It was time, in short, to be up and doing; even if for the present it could only be in the way of perhaps catching a glimpse of that strange and, he suspected, sinister fellow with the mutilated left hand.

Marco, the grandson of Andreas, and his friends had established that he habitually drank before lunch in a place called the Bar Democratico in one of the calli off the main street. This, in fact, was all the information which Marco had produced in the last two days; although Annunzietta had come in with an extraordinary tale that the young lady who had gone to the Ca' Vespucci now claimed to be a descendant of a very ancient and noble family and that the old woman, who was well known to be a little foolish, was quite taken in by her. Annunzietta said the whole of Venice was talking about it; and getting ready to laugh.

The whole of Venice, d'Espinal considered, was a sizeable exaggeration. But there was no doubt that the story itself stank of fraud. Equally there was no doubt that it was connected somehow with the supposed Botticelli; though whether it might or might not also have anything to do with the man Vespe was unknown for the moment. One could only pray that he might find some light, guidance or inspiration in the Bar Democratico. But he did not seriously think he would.

It was a dark place with old political posters on the walls and smoky photographs of heavily armed, bearded and on the whole, d'Espinal considered, extremely unpleasant looking young men dressed in semi-military uniform; a glittering coffee machine rumbling quietly, a smell of wine and pasta and half a dozen bare plastic tables. Vespe was clearly not over choice in his tastes. Nor was the welcome any more promising. One man sitting alone, three others about some card game and the barman in shirt sleeves and jeans, all stopped short in a noisy argument and stared at him as he entered. For a moment, as he confessed to Paolo afterward, he felt damned uncomfortable but he beamed round at them, wished them 'Buon giorno' in the clumsiest possible Italian, and in English asked for a glass of white vino.

He lingered over it obstinately, leaning against the high counter, while the silence grew oppressive. At least, for what it was worth, he had come to the right bar. The solitary one was Vespe, and exactly as Marco had described him. Two fingers only on the left hand with what was certainly a big diamond flashing on one of them, an expensive suit, probably of Swiss cut, and carelessly worn. At one time perhaps hard and lean but now running to fat, cropped iron coloured hair, a viciously tight mouth and abnormally pale grey eyes like cold flints. Well in his fifties, d'Espinal thought, but still a dangerous brute; he wondered briefly what this type of animal had to do with the Ca' Vespucci and Isola San Giorgio. The man was watching him, and he finished his wine and turned back to the counter saying, 'Buono. Molto excellente. Encore, again...'

Vespe said in Italian, 'Tell that bastard bullfrog son of a camel to get out of here.'

D'Espinal felt his colour rising, took a deep breath and held it, and watched the white wine slopping into his glass again, while the barman laughed. 'His money's good,' the man answered reasonably. 'It's better than yours. With all you have you don't push too much out.'

One of the others guffawed and then stopped short and muttered, 'No, now, Giacomo; we can't drive the tourists away. You millionaires don't know the way it goes.'

'Since when did you learn to lick spittle?' Vespe asked.

There was a tight silence until d'Espinal demanded plaintively, 'What are they saying? I only want to know how to get to the church of San Pietro.'

Vespe laughed then and still in Italian said, 'Churches and nuns and fat priests, that's all they ever think about. There was a time when we thought to rid the world of all of them. We had guts in our bellies those days.'

Again no one spoke until another of the three card players half whispered, 'There's a story that you did your best at San Stefano, Giacomo...'

Vespe's face drained almost as pale as his eyes and for a moment he seemed to stiffen in on himself. He half pushed himself up, but at the same time the barman brought his hand down flat on the wet zinc counter top with a vicious slap. He roared, 'Now, by God, have done with it. You...' He shook his closed fingers at Vespe. 'You are about no good here in Venice and I want no part of it. I am the one man who is not afraid of you, Giacomo Vespe...' Once again it was quiet and turning back to d'Espinal he went on, suddenly in surprising Cockney English, 'Signore, please to drink your wine and go. My friends are old partisans and they still fight forgotten battles. The Church of San Pietro is that way, along the Fondamenta di Sant' Anna. Only please to go.'

Outside in the sunshine d'Espinal realized that he was sweating slightly. A man of some urbanity himself he had found that brief experience disturbing; although whether it also had any other significance was by no means clear. But what became very certain was that if the undesirable person, Vespe, did indeed have some connection with this business it introduced an ugly and dangerous element. One could scarcely imagine that the fellow had any great concern for art, but there could be very little doubt that he was a murderous rascal.

D'Espinal was still pondering on this when, after a long lunch at the Danieli, he returned to Paolo's garden. Andreas was sleeping peacefully on one of the old marble benches with the cat, Isabella d'Este, sitting beside him and staring haughtily at the stone lions. In the shade of the balcony Niccolo Machiavelli appeared to be contemplating some more than usually devious piece of diplomacy; and Paolo himself, with his glasses perched askew on his nose, was dozing over a book. He opened one eye and murmured, 'Well, Harcourt?'

D'Espinal sat down gratefully. 'Not very. What is the book which appears to fascinate you so much?'

'Old Rutilio Lenardi. Speaking of him the other day made me think of it again. He spent most of his life trying to find the key to the ancient Etruscan language. And this is the total result, which he presented to me.' Paolo pushed the book away. 'I recall that Arturo Vespucci came here after the old gentleman's death to ask me something about it. But I cannot now recollect what it was. Did you have a successful morning?'

D'Espinal brooded over the dappled green and gold of the trees against the old rose brick building across the canal. 'I observed an evil and violent man,' he said heavily. 'And I am a little frightened.'

It was quiet in the big room. At this time of the afternoon the sun struck slantwise on the canal outside and flung back through the windows a wavering reflection of greenish light, which danced and rippled steadily over the ceiling and down the walls while Simone worked on steadily and alone. She had first of all that morning written to Frau Meisner in Munich and then, by checking through the dated and addressed envelopes, she had established an outline of Arturo Vespucci's activities from 1959 to November 1962.

Plotting them systematically in variously coloured inks on a big map of Central Italy, one simple conclusion—perhaps too simple, she suspected—had appeared. That Arturo's journeys looked inevitably like a gradual closing in on something. For 1959 there was a single black line from Genoa down the coast to Piombino, back to Pisa and then inland to Florence; a journey such as anyone interested in the Cattaneo family might have made, and what he had referred to in the first draft of his book as the 'pilgrimage'. In 1960 there was not so much material, it covered only three weeks, and on the map it came out as a green circle around Florence.

But in 1961 he had made three trips. In April to Florence again; in July a round tour which made a rough oval from Florence to Arezzo, on to Citta di Castello, north to San Sepolcro and back by way of Bibbiena to Florence once more. And finally, in September, he had started back at Arezzo and moved on to San Sepolcro, taken in a place which now appeared for the first time, Pieve San Stefano, and then returned to Arezzo. At that stage the pattern had still looked meaningless, merely a series of visits to places most of which were only names to Simone; although she knew they were historic towns as old as the hills among which they were built. But there was still a suggestion of purpose about it; and, what was perhaps even more important, it was between April and July of this year that Arturo had started putting his notes into cipher.

The last year was to clinch it. Working from the envelopes there were only two lines in 1962. The first in June and July, beginning and ending in Arezzo, had repeated the circle of San Sepolcro, Pieve San Stefano, Bagno and Bibbiena; and the last, in November, which literally was Arturo Vespucci's final journey, was just a ring around San Sepolcro and a route out to Cesena and Forli—the quickest way back to Venice. It proved nothing really, Simone thought; but at least it suggested that he had found the Botticelli in this area and, most probably, in San Sepolcro itself.

It proved nothing, Simone told herself again. What she now had to find was the incident or discovery which had made Arturo Vespucci realize that what he was tracing was no longer just the material for a rather speculative book about Simonetta, but something infinitely more important; something so important that it had caused him to switch quite suddenly from Italian to a deliberate and carefully consistent cipher, a form of letter substitution in which he had used a series of curious angular symbols. The characters looked tantalizingly familiar; simple shapes which you might expect to see cut in stone or wax, and not unlike a type of primitive Greek. There was no doubt they made up an alphabet of sorts; but for the present she could not recognize it, and merely guessing or experimenting with frequencies could well be so much wasted time. She turned back firmly to the notes in clear.

Arturo appeared to be a man who had thought on to the paper, writing down questions as they occurred to him and going back to them later with the answers, often with pure speculation. It became a sort of loose diary not only of his movements but of his ideas by the way, and to Simone it suggested a restless, perhaps undisciplined, but aggressive and sometimes penetrating mind; as pure research she considered rather primly, it was loose and unsystematic. But in 1960, the year he did the least work, a significant change appeared.

He was in Florence then and still only collecting material for the book on Simonetta; but after descriptions of her tomb, her lesser known portrait in the Church of All Saints, and his own somewhat unconventional views on the Botticelli Venus and the Primavera, he quoted an extract from a letter of Botticelli himself. "Now did my princely master entreat me to paint for him a likeness of his beloved mistress; that he might convey it privately into his chamber and there worship her in secret ..." That was new to Simone and there was no indication of where Arturo had got it, and she muttered irritably, 'Slapdash again; why can't the man refer to his sources?'

This seemed to have fascinated him and he came back to it time after time. "It can only have been Giuliano de' Medici," he wrote, "certainly not Lorenzo, and if Giuliano the portrait must have been Simonetta..." That also was a guess, Simone thought. But then he had gone on, "According to accredited dates Primavera was painted two years after she died, Birth of Venus nine, Mars and Venus for the Vespucci family, now National Gallery London, nine again. Picture at Frankfurt date doubtful; also doubtful if it is Simonetta. Piero di Cosimo painted the Chantilly picture three years after her death. It isn't possible, no artist can carry the memory of a face so long as that, not even Simonetta's. There must have been a master portrait. So where is it?"

'Now,' Simone murmured approvingly, 'he really does have something interesting there. If true,' she added dubiously.

He went on with slightly acid notes covering talks with people in Florence—irritatingly named only by initials—most of whom, it appeared, had more or less politely laughed at him. Then, with a sour touch of his own business instinct, he asked, "Could it be one of the pictures Botticelli is supposed to have burned when he got converted to Savonarola? But how could it? It wasn't his to burn. Giuliano must have given good money for that job, Botticelli was one of the highest paid artists of his day; admitted Giuliano himself was dead by then, but his possessions would go back to the family, including his pictures. Botticelli had no claim; he must have got his money long before. The Medici were bankers and whoever heard of a banker giving up anything once he's paid for it? I ought to know."

Towards the end of that period he said, "Suppose it went to the Vespucci instead of the Medici; suppose they bought it?"

'Speculation again,' Simone sighed. 'You really will have to get out of this habit, Arturo, if we're to do any good.'

"I'm going to find it," he announced. "It's only an idea, and a cracked idea so the experts say. But I made five millions out of following ideas. After five hundred years it's all a guessing game and my guess is as good as theirs..."

The remaining notes for 1960 were written on conventional foolscap paper. From the Ca' Vespucci early in November he had taken Becky to Cannes for the winter, observing "Becky loves this place; she'd sooner be here than Venice". He himself had travelled on north to Chantilly, apparently to look at the Piero di Cosimo portrait there, and he had written, "Makes Simonetta look insipid. Don't like that viper coiled round her neck; supposed to be symbolic of the illness which killed her. And was her hair as red as that?" Returning to Cannes with a violent chill he had then wanted to fly to Frankfurt to see the Botticelli in the Kunstinstitut, but Becky had refused to let him go. He had remarked, "She fusses too much; I don't intend to die before I've finished this job." By then he was a man in the grip of an obsession.

Simone closed that folder slowly, and with an involuntary feeling of tragedy—what Becky might have called a goose walking over her grave—sat quite still looking at it for a few seconds before reaching out for the next three; those covering 1961. The year he had changed to the cipher; the year, she thought, that he had discovered there really was another picture somewhere.

The first few sheets again were ordinary foolscap —which she was now starting to associate with his working here in this room—and Arturo started abruptly, "Supper with old Lenardi last night. Worried about him, he's looking very frail after the winter. Took him half a dozen of good burgundy and he said, 'I hope I might have time to drink it 'Turo.' I can't afford to lose him. He's hanging on until his book comes out. I told him we'd rather have him with us than the best of books about a long dead language and he said I should talk, I was more than half in love with a long dead girl myself...'

At this point the door opened and Simone started violently, blinking round at Maria coming in with a tray and china and tea. The maid's dark eyes flicked at the papers on the desk, and rested on Simone's rumpled hair and a long dark smudge of dust across her face with professional disapproval. She said,

'Those things should have been well cleaned. I will have it done.'

'If you don't mind,' Simone answered. 'I want them left just as they are.'

Maria stared at her for a moment as if prepared to argue but then murmured, 'It must be as you wish, of course.' She added, 'I have to go out. Will you object if Alberto takes away the tray when you're finished?'

'Alberto,' Simone repeated. 'That reminds me; Alberto always seems to be about,' and added absently, already peering back at something Arturo had written, "Rather have him with us than the best of books about a long dead language". What language? she wondered with her private thrill of excitement again; what long dead language? But she said, 'Every time I open a door Alberto's just around the corner somewhere.'

Maria stiffened, watching Simone frowning at Arturo Vespucci's papers. 'Does the signorina complain?' she asked formally.

'Not really,' Simone murmured. 'I just thought it was curious. It doesn't matter.'

At this time of the afternoon the big campo was almost deserted. On the left it was open to a rio called the Canal of the Beggars, with old houses and boat yards on the other bank, and on its far side it was closed in by the marble façade of the hospital and the towers of the great Church of Saints John and Paul—now flaming burnt orange against a dark blue sky. It was hot and quiet; there were only a few pigeons bobbing in their own shadows, a group of ladies earnestly studying the Colleoni Statue, and an old man in blue trousers and a yellow straw hat surrounded by glowing baskets of flowers and dozing peacefully under a sunshade on the other side of the square.

Miss Pentecost waited patiently outside the small café on the shady side. She watched a barge slide past noiselessly; and then a funeral procession rowing out to San Michele, with a standing priest and an arch of scarlet gladioli supported by two dark figures. The women around the statue scurried across to the water steps to watch it pass, and a solitary gondolier sitting there took off his hat for a moment. Then it was quiet again, until the pigeons flapped up suddenly at the sound of heels clicking impatiently across the pavestones. They stopped at Miss Pentecost's table, and she said, 'You're late.'

'It was inconvenient to come at all,' Maria answered. 'I have more work now there are two of them to attend.'

She was not complaining. Maria was unhesitatingly competent about her trade; as she would be with her own interests, Miss Pentecost thought. She studied the correct, tailored suit and white silk blouse and asked, 'Tea?'

'I do not have time.' Maria waved the waiter away sharply and sat down; 'Why did you call me? What is going wrong?'

'Nothing. Or not much. You understood about the girl?'

Maria smiled briefly. 'She will be well looked after. Alberto takes kindly to the work. But you understand if she makes some move herself we cannot stop her?'

'So long as we know what she does; who she meets.'

'What is going wrong?' Maria asked again.

Miss Pentecost took out and lit a cigarette, replacing the lighter in her handbag before she answered. 'Signora Teestock now feels that we shall not find it easy ... to control her.'

'And if we do not?'

'Isn't that obvious? Signora Teestock,' Miss Pentecost said carefully, 'is becoming nervous. Not so far as to give up, not yet; but she is worried.' Across the square there were people trying to buy flowers from the old man; one of them was shaking him and he stirred lazily, yawning and grumbling. Maria watched them while Miss Pentecost went on, 'She says Signorina Greenwood will swear there was a real picture; and real emeralds.'

Still watching the old flower seller Maria said, 'There is that danger. So we must think of something for Miss Greenwood.'

'Signora Teestock says no harm must come to her. If there's any danger of that she'll stop everything. She might even warn the principessa.'

'Who has yet suggested any harm? So what do you propose?'

Miss Pentecost looked down at the tip of her cigarette. 'We shall go on, of course. But we must make it so that nobody in Venice will believe a word Miss Greenwood says. You have already put it about that she claims to be a descendant of the Vespucci and Medici?' Maria nodded and Emilia went on, 'You might whisper she realizes already that the picture is a forgery but does not say so to the principessa because it would not be profitable. One can think of dozens of things. The principessa gives her money; a great deal of money. You could hint to the principessa that she needs a dress for the reception.'

'As indeed she does,' Maria announced, her professional instincts apparently coming uppermost suddenly. 'She has not brought anything suitable with her. Imagine, to come to Venice, to a house like ours, without at least one formal gown.'

'So take her to Donnabella's; where Mrs Medina-Silvestro gets her clothes, though one would never think so to look at her. Have the principessa get her something expensive and see that the girls there talk about it. It's all quite easy.'

'Very easy.' Maria's face was expressionless. 'If it is enough.'

'It must be enough,' Miss Pentecost answered sharply. 'All we want is to be rid of her once she's done her part. She must simply go back to London.'

Maria smiled briefly. 'That would be best. But one thing must be certain. That we shall not give up.' She reached out for her handbag. 'I must go. Is there anything more?'

'Only one thing. The person who is to deal with the picture is here. You might find him entertaining. He's a big man; quite imposing, but a fool. And he imagines he is irresistible to women.'

'Don't they all?'

'This one more than most. The point is, Maria, he must see the portrait to make his plans. He says that's essential. Can you arrange it?'

Maria eyed her speculatively but asked, 'Why not? It will be a pleasure to deal with a man again. Very well. On Thursday they go to the theatre; they are to leave at eight. Have him come to our staff entrance at nine o'clock exactly. I will be waiting for him.' She got up. 'I must hurry now.'

'He will probably ask you a great many questions.'

'Which I shall know how to answer.' There was a flicker of amusement in Maria's eyes; 'Signorina Pentecost, I have never yet trusted any man; though I sometimes allow them to amuse me.'

Her heels clicked sharply across the square once more and Miss Pentecost sat on long enough to finish her cigarette, watching the old man across the square now settling down to doze among his flowers again. It had to work out this way, she told herself; it was inconceivable that any normal young woman could face the barrage of laughter and disbelief that Venice would turn on Simone Greenwood if she ever tried to tell the truth. At last she got up and started back slowly along the hot footwalk on the Canal of the Beggars; she thought suddenly of trying to find d'Espinal in his cool green garden, said aloud, 'Don't be a fool,' and went on steadily towards the waterfront where Pietro would be waiting with the boat to take her back to San Giorgio.

CHAPTER SIX

Simone had started work early, certain by now that she was very close to the discovery which had changed Arturo's rather wild speculations into something like historical certainty. She had examined all his arguments as critically as they would be examined when they were published, and she was prepared to accept that the known commemorative pictures of Simonetta, the Birth of Venus, Primavera and Mars and Venus, were painted from two to nine years after her death. She was willing to grant that Botticelli must have executed at least one other portrait for Giuliano de' Medici during Simonetta's lifetime; although she still had not traced the letter which Arturo had quoted. She would admit too that it was at least possible for such a portrait to have served as a master copy for later works; this, as she knew, being a quite respectable practice of that period. Tintoretto for instance, as Arturo himself pointed out, had used the Sleeping Cupid of Michelangelo in one of his own pictures. But to argue that this of itself proved the existence of the earlier study was too much. At the best it was no more than an interesting theory; until the last days of Arturo's visit to Florence in April 1961.

His notes at this time, the last he had made in Italian, were tired and discouraged. It looked as if the idea was burning itself out, and after a further series of frustrated searches, a fruitless examination of such documents as he could get access to—the Catalogue of 1498, the Collection of Isabella d'Este, and the Inventory of 1542—he wrote, "Beginning to think I'm up against a dead end everywhere; sure I'm right but can't break through." He had heard also, in a letter from Becky, that Rutilio Lenardi was now ill; and he was feeling far from well himself. At that stage he had been defeated; but he still said, "Get back home and rest and think this out again."

After that, written carefully on uniform foolscap sheets and therefore almost certainly back here in Venice, he had switched abruptly into cipher; and a cipher which obviously he could not have invented and learned to use in a few hours. It was written neatly and clearly and it suggested Arturo's obsessive secrecy and his own special kind of determination. It suggested also, Simone thought—in fact she had now been thinking it for several days—an archaic alphabet; one she did not recognize and therefore a specialist study. And that, she thought, inevitably tied up with one of Arturo's earlier notes; about Rutilio Lenardi. "Rather have him with us than the best of books about a long dead language."

'It might be guessing again, Arturo,' she muttered. 'And one of us doing that's quite enough. But I've got to find that book.'

She sat back staring across the room. But she already knew at least the title of every volume here. They were mostly histories of the Medici, of the Vespucci, a set of Vasari's *Lives of the Painters* and studies of the Renaissance from which Arturo had helped himself to liberal extracts. There was certainly nothing by Lenardi. And of course there would not be; neither here nor anywhere in the house. If Arturo had been so secretive as not even to tell his own wife what he had discovered, he certainly would never be careless enough to put it into cipher and then leave the key lying around for anyone to see.

'There must be a copy of it somewhere in Venice,' she said, and took off her glasses to go restlessly across to the window. Down below the backwater canal was dark green and quiet—she had never yet seen even a gondola passing along it—and for a moment she pictured Arturo coming back here so furtively in the darkness and mist of a November night, stealing up that canal in a quietened launch with these things which Becky still swore had cost him his life. And which she half imagined might yet cost others. 'Getting fanciful again,' Simone said briskly and turned back to the desk to take up the letter file.

The two letters from museums describing other portraits were not all that important. The other from the Musée Condé refusing austerely to discuss the value of the unique book known as the *Very Rich Hours of the Duc de Berry*, was curious chiefly because it seemed to be irrelevant and because it was dated December 1962. Thinking of Becky's mysterious reference the other day to something which she appeared to imagine was particularly unlucky, which Simonetta herself might have had in her hands as she lay dying, Simone considered that for a time before she passed on to the last two letters. The one from Frau Meisner, and the rough note.

It was a page torn from a note book, the paper

was poor and coarse and already turning brown and becoming brittle with age. Originally it had been folded very small and then crumpled at some time, and it was covered on both sides with a hurried fine scribble in pencil, smudged and in parts almost completely obliterated. What little she could recognize was again in Italian but the individual characters, she thought, were rather more angular in form than Italian people themselves usually write. It looked like a letter by a man using his second language.

At first she could only make out a few words here and there, sometimes no more than groups of letters; but, working on a sheet of lined paper, she transcribed these separately as nearly as possible to their same relative positions as in the original note. Some combinations were easy, others remained tantalizingly elusive, and occasionally a phrase had disappeared almost completely. Conscious of a growing excitement again, a certainty that if this itself was not what had caused Arturo to switch his notes into cipher it was at least very close to it, she nevertheless worked on methodically all through the morning; picking out a fresh word and then another, a few letters, sometimes only one or two. Once she made an obvious mistake and swore quietly; at some point the door opened and Alberto appeared murmuring, 'Coffee, signorina,' and she barked, 'Go away!' But at last, exhausted with concentration, she sighed and leaned back, closing and screwing up her eyes.

She whispered, 'Well, Arturo; we've got it. Some of it. But where did it come from, and how much more is there?'

The letter was still far from complete but there

was quite enough now, and Simone reached out for her typewriter and started to translate deliberately and carefully. It read "... old friend; in great haste and danger ... Would not do this but I believe ... of hell and can think of nothing better." There was a complete phrase missing there, but it went on "... attack soon and clear we cannot hold. There are things here which must not be allowed to fall .. belong Italy and Italian people, this you will understand when you see what they are." Another sentence had gone and it started again, "... and boy who swears he can get through. Send this before by ... so you will be ready for them. Hide them well, old friend, and God go with you. May He give it to us both to drink wine together again some day. Trudi also would wish me to give her love..."

'So that,' Simone said, 'must be Paul Meisner. That's the only person it can be. But for heaven's sake...' she glared malevolently at Arturo's cipher, 'how much more is there in this stuff?'

She was starting to make a precise copy of some of the curious script when the princess bustled in 'Here now, love,' Becky started, 'Maria says you were down here before eight. And you sent your coffee back. You don't want to go at it like that, you know. It'll keep.'

'Mmm?' Simone answered. She stared at the princess, coming back to the present, and added, 'Becky, we're getting on now. And we should know more when Frau Meisner answers my letter.'

'Where we've got to get,' Becky interrupted firmly, 'is along to the shops.' She had changed considerably in the last few days, but just for a moment a trace of her former uneasiness appeared again as she went on, 'Maria says you didn't bring a long dress with you. She just happened to mention it.'

'But don't you want to know about this?' Simone asked.

'I know you young girls don't drag a lot of clothes around with you these days,' Becky hurried on. 'It's all nylon and nothing. So we shall have to do something about it, and we don't have a lot of time. Do pay attention, child!'

'I said don't you want to know?' Simone repeated obstinately.

'Eh? Of course I do, love. But it'll keep until we're having lunch. Maria was saying that as we've got to be quick about it the best place is Donnabella's. So I told her she'd better come with us.'

'I'm not quite sure what we're talking about.'

'A party dress for you, girl. And you'll have to let me see to it; don't let's be silly.' Simone started to say something but, rather like a sharp but affectionate grandmother, the princess cut in again. 'If it comes to that we haven't said a breath nor word about what to pay you, doing all this work for me.'

'No,' Simone admitted. 'I haven't thought about it.'

'Well you should. You'll never make a fortune if you go on that way; you'll have to have one left you. Where I come from we've got a right old saying, "If thee does owt for nowt, do it for thysen".' Becky paused and then finished quickly, 'So we'll call it a hundred pounds a week, that's about a hundred and seventy thousand lire.'

'But Becky,' Simone protested, 'that's far too much.'

'I'm the best judge of that. My Arthur always

used to say if you want quality you must expect to pay for it and then it's a compliment to both sides. But if you want to be independent we'll call it a hundred and fifty thousand. I'm a smart old business woman myself.'

At that point Maria came in. Simone was not quite certain, but she thought that for a moment she caught something in the conspiratorial eyes; satisfaction or even a hint of triumph. Maria murmured, 'Madame, I have told them at Donnabella's to be ready for us at twelve o'clock.'

'Let's be off then,' the princess said. 'Come on now, love,' she added to Simone. 'I haven't had a lot of fun lately.'

Alberto seemed to materialize immediately when Simone left Becky after lunch. He appeared again, wedged patiently against the rails on the water bus from the Rialto, apparently watching the sparkling panorama of the Grand Canal like Simone herself. When they reached the Accademia he waited politely for her to step ashore before following; and half an hour later as she came out of the great building itself he was still there in the shade of the entrance archway. She asked herself rather wildly, 'Is he just fascinated, or what?' staring at him as she passed, to which he answered with a faintly bashful grin and a curious little half bow. But, once more, he was only a few yards behind her as she crossed the square and then the bridge and plunged in among the strolling crowd drifting towards St Mark's.

As she had been directed from the Accademia Library she went straight to the big bookshop on the corner of the square, and when at last she came out again Alberto was still under the colonnade, studying a window display of glittering Murano glassware. This time Simone stopped firmly. She asked, 'Alberto; why are you following me?'

'Why, signorina?' He did not appear to know himself and hesitated as if he was searching his mind both for a reason and for words. He started, 'Signorina Maria...' and finished with an air of sudden relief, 'it is the custom of the house.' Simone stared at him and he explained, 'When the principessa walks out she is always attended. One might be molested,' he tried.

'In Venice; in daylight? What complete nonsense.' He looked hurt, and she went on quickly, 'All right, Alberto; one might be molested.' She studied him thoughtfully for a moment and then said, 'But not on the water I hope; so you can find me a gondola now.' That seemed to please him and he answered, 'By your favour; if you will follow me.' In a few minutes he brought her out surprisingly on to the Grand Canal again and she told him flatly, 'Now, Alberto, I'm going alone. If you choose to wait here for me you may. But I might be quite a long time.'

She left him at the landing stage looking vaguely like a deserted spaniel; and surely far more worried than he should have been over such a small thing. It was curious and slightly irritating, it looked like Maria being officious again, and Simone waited until the gondolier had edged well out from the steps before glancing again at the address which the middle-aged woman assistant in the bookshop had given her and saying, 'The gallery of Signor Paolo Raffaele, off the Rio della Toletta.'

They went back past the Accademia again, and

then through a maze of progressively quieter canals until the unexpected garden appeared, sleepy in the afternoon sunlight. There was a very elderly man, with a face like a cheerful slightly mischievous walnut, dozing on a stone seat but he blinked up at the sound of her footsteps, and she asked, 'Signor Raffaele?' Looking at her with evident approval he said, 'The padrone? If the signorina will be pleased to follow me?' and pushed himself up, creaking slightly. 'Don't bother,' Simone told him quickly, but he answered, 'I insist,' and led her to the foot of the steps.

There were two men and two cats sitting silently up on the balcony. One with a shock of white hair and a thoughtful face, with a look of being almost a part of the old house himself, who was clearly the scholar. His companion was a big man who stared at her as she appeared, giving a strange, momentary impression of uneasy recognition, before she said, 'Signor Paolo Raffaele? I'm sorry to disturb you.'

'It is my pleasure,' the older one replied. He too seemed surprised, and there was a little silence until the other got up quickly saying, 'Pardon me,' and dragging another cane chair forward.

'I ought not to burst in without an introduction,' Simone started, 'you won't know me. I'm Simone Greenwood.'

'It's most kind of you to visit us. May I present Mr Harcourt d'Espinal?'

The name tugged at Simone's memory. And then she remembered Miss Pentecost, on the stairs to her own office in London, asking, 'Have you ever met a man named d'Espinal?' She looked at him again but before she could speak he announced, 'Miss

Greenwood and I have already observed each other. But as from a distance.'

'Of course,' Simone said, 'on the aeroplane coming over.' There was something about him which puzzled her, uneasiness where you would have expected a man of that appearance to be unfailingly urbane. She went on, 'You must know Miss Pentecost. She mentioned you; in London.'

His face turned extraordinarily blank. 'Did she indeed? It was uncommonly kind of her.' For a moment, like Alberto, he appeared to be searching for an answer. 'We do have some slight acquaintance.'

Paolo was stroking one of the cats. He murmured, 'Cesare Borgia, Miss Greenwood. That swaggering fellow there is Benvenuto Cellini.'

Simone stared at them both and d'Espinal protested, 'Come now, Paolo, you'll have Miss Greenwood feeling that we're a pair of very odd fellows. And I'm sure she has far more weighty concerns than your cats.'

She said, 'I'm looking for a book by a man named Rutilio Lenardi.' D'Espinal's chair creaked suddenly but neither of them spoke and she went on, 'I tried at the Accademia Library, but it was rather difficult because I couldn't tell them much about it. Except it would be a study of an early language of some kind.'

Paolo nodded gently. 'Etruscan.'

'You know?' she asked quickly. 'I hoped you might. The Accademia sent me on to a Signorina Sabbioni at the bookshop in St Mark's Square.'

'That would be Caterina Sabbioni. She was Rutilio's secretary.'

'Yes. She knew all about it. She told me it was called *A Study of the Ancient Etruscan*. And she remembered that Signor Lenardi had presented copies to just two people in Venice. To a Mr Arturo Vespucci. And you.' D'Espinal was sitting with his eyes half closed, but he glanced at Simone quickly, and she went on, 'I can't find Arturo Vespucci's copy, and I rather badly need to look at that book. I want the Etruscan characters.'

Paolo nodded again. 'Nothing could be simpler. Pardon me one moment.' He lifted the cat Borgia down gently, got up and went into the house through the big windows.

With his finger tips placed together, chin on his chest and eyelids drooping, pouting slightly, d'Espinal appeared to be pondering heavily. Without looking at Simone he repeated softly, 'Ancient Etruscan. You will acquit me of any unseemly curiosity, I hope, but such a dry dusty subject. You're engaged in research perhaps?'

'I'm working on some papers.'

'Concerning the late Arturo Vespucci?'

'Left by him.' Simone stopped suddenly, looking at d'Espinal. 'How did you know that?'

'You mentioned his name. It was a simple connection.'

'I make a point,' she told him rather primly, 'of never discussing my client's business.'

'How very correct,' he agreed. 'I am properly rebuked.'

'I didn't mean that,' Simone said quickly. 'I'm sorry. In fact I hope you'll be able to read the whole thing one day. It's an astonishing story. But just for the present...'

'But just for the present you feel there are wheels within wheels, as it were, and choose to preserve a proper diplomacy. You must forgive an idle fellow who has nothing better to do than ask tiresome questions.'

Before Simone could answer that Paolo came back with the book. He seemed to be faintly amused. 'You are a student of archaic scripts?'

'Not usually this far back,' Simone answered. 'May I?' she said, and perched her heavy glasses on her nose to turn over the pages, while d'Espinal watched her with something like fascination on his face.

'May one enquire,' he asked, 'the precise significance of the Etruscan?'

Simone hesitated; but she could scarcely expect to borrow this book without at least explaining why she wanted it, and she said, 'It just happens that some of the notes I'm transcribing appear to be written in these characters.'

'They are as secret as that?' d'Espinal asked.

'Secret?' She frowned at him. 'I didn't say so; I don't know yet.' Then turning back to the book she breathed suddenly, 'That's it; exactly what I want.' There were two inset pages of alphabets and a series of photographs of characters cut in stone or clay. 'I knew it,' she went on triumphantly. 'I knew they were incised letters. And I knew some of them were like primitive Greek.'

Paolo apparently was still mildly amused, but d'Espinal stared at her as if she was something the like of which he had never seen before. He watched her in silence for a time before asking, 'Miss Greenwood; among your other manifest abilities are you also an art expert?'

She shook her head, saying, 'No more than most people,' but looked up at him sharply. 'Why?'

He seemed to be uncomfortable again. 'Why indeed? Merely another pointless curiosity.'

'I'm being abominably rude,' Simone confessed. 'Bursting in on you, borrowing this, and getting so mysterious. Only I can't tell what it might lead to yet; it could be something quite startling. But just for the present I really don't know how far I'm free to talk about it.' She got up. 'If you don't mind...'

'You wish to be about your work?' Paolo smiled. 'Please take the book for as long as you need it. I make only one condition; that when you feel you may you will satisfy our curiosity.'

Simone laughed, a little breathlessly. 'I'll do that, I promise. I can't think of a better place to tell it in.'

'You are very kind,' Paolo told her, and d'Espinal announced, 'If you will permit, Miss Greenwood, I will come a little way with you.'

He was puzzled and perturbed. The Pentecost, he remembered, had said that this young woman was to make the whole project possible. At the moment he did not see how, but if she was to be used as an innocent tool he did not care for it at all; there was now a hint of danger creeping into this thing, he thought, besides the original smell of wickedness. On the other hand Miss Greenwood was patently no simpleton; and if she was actually claiming to be a descendant of the Vespucci that too might be part of the whole devious stratagem. The devil of it was that quite clearly she was not prepared to give anything away.

When they came out on the canal he said, 'I fear

we shall not find a gondola for you here.'

'It doesn't matter,' Simone told him. 'I only took one before because I was being followed.'

D'Espinal stopped dead. 'You were what?'

She looked surprised and then laughed. 'It's nothing sinister; only in the Ca' Vespucci they seem to have some rather eighteenth-century ideas. They think a woman shouldn't go out unattended; they send a footman with you.'

'I see. I think I see. A charming old custom.'

'But irritating. I told Alberto that I'd meet him again where I left him.' They walked on and she asked suddenly, 'You do know Miss Pentecost, don't you?'

D'Espinal's face turned blank again. 'As I said; some slight acquaintance. I doubt,' he added ponderously, 'that anyone really knows Miss Pentecost. Perhaps not even Miss Pentecost herself.'

'That sounds somewhat cryptic.'

'Did it so? It was meant to be profound ... We turn left now. Before us we perceive the Rio di San Trovaso. And here you may observe the famous old boat yard much painted by Francesco Guardi.'

'And you are remarkably adroit at changing the subject.'

'I had thought it was exhausted. We now cross this bridge. If you continue that way and take the Calle Gambaro on the right you will emerge at the Accademia.'

Simone considered him for a moment, smiling slightly, and then held out her hand. 'Goodbye. And you don't want to talk about Miss Pentecost.'

'I should be delighted to talk about the lady,' he announced. 'If I knew what to say. But for yourself, Miss Greenwood, I take an apéritif each day outside Quadri's on the Piazza. Twelve o'clock will always find me there. I imagine,' he added modestly, 'that you can scarcely miss me. And when you take a gondola you should look for Marco who works from the Sant' Angelo steps. He is the grandson of old Andreas at the gallery.'

'It's very good of you,' Simone said slowly. 'But why?'

D'Espinal assumed his most pontifical look. 'Even in Venice another friend is sometimes useful.'

She looked slightly puzzled but thanked him again solemnly, and he watched her walking alongside the canal, waited for her to turn off into the calle, and then started back himself. In the garden again Paolo was still sitting lazily exactly as they had left him, and d'Espinal asked, 'In God's Holy Name, Paolo, what d'you make of that? You observed the likeness?'

'It was there, I thought; yes.'

'Paolo.' D'Espinal leaned forward. 'Is it possible, even remotely possible, that she is indeed a descendant of the Vespucci?'

'My dear boy... Not even remotely.'

'Then how d'you explain the story—which Annunzietta says is now all over Venice—that she claims to be?'

'Quite simply. The likeness supports the claim; and both are being used in some way to impose on the Princess Kodaly, who is said to be a singularly gullible old person. That young lady would never be foolish enough to claim something so incredible without a very precise reason. In your English expression, she has her head screwed on the right way.'

'Yet she looks honest.'

Paolo sighed. 'I learned long ago not to trust any woman by her appearance; no more than I would an egg by its shell. Not until she reaches Annunzietta's age and even then only with misgiving.'

'But what is she doing?'

'She is extracting a very considerable fee and a pleasant life in Venice from the Kodaly—Annunzietta says they are seen everywhere together and it is noticed that the princess always pays—on the pretext of deciphering those notes of Arturo Vespucci. Which are themselves almost certainly quite worthless.'

'Your cynicism belies your kindly nature, old friend. I can see more. A few days ago the Pentecost admitted they had no provenance of the picture; but she said they might find it. What does that suggest?'

'Ah yes, the Pentecost...' Paolo interrupted.

'Let me finish. It suggests that is what this young person is here to trace. And if she does? Whatever her own private plans might be, if she finds indisputable proof that the picture is indeed a Botticelli, and if it is subsequently purloined, what then? What happens, Paolo? She becomes a dangerous witness. And,' he added heavily, 'the lot of a dangerous witness in the matter of something which might well be worth a million pounds or more is precarious to say the least. Devilish precarious.'

Paolo sighed again. 'The picture cannot be a Botticelli. Your San Giorgio women are deluding themselves; and you too. And Miss Pentecost...'

'Be damned to Miss Pentecost. If she's not already. Which I regard as highly probable.' D'Espinal relapsed into his now habitual brooding attitude and muttered, 'I am confused, Paolo. But I see now why that woman warned me not to approach the girl. And it appears also that she is under a form of surveillance.'

'Surveillance?' Paolo asked. 'What do you mean?'

'She is followed everywhere; apparently by some fellow of the household. She seems to take it lightly enough. For my own part, I do not. I tell you, Paolo, that young woman is in some danger. And if by chance one could save her from it she might in simple gratitude tell us how much she knows. I have therefore somewhat obliquely instructed the young woman that we are, as it were, available if necessary.'

'Was that advisable?' Paolo asked. 'I am a trifle elderly for Perseus; and you, one fears, are a little too fat.' D'Espinal gazed at him reproachfully, but he went on, 'About Miss Pentecost. She telephoned a few minutes since, and she requires you to call her back; about some appointment she has arranged for you. And,' he added with a touch of malice, 'she made it unmistakably an order.'

D'Espinal glowered. He said darkly, 'Paolo, I have already told that creature to beware lest she fall into error.'

On St Mark's Square the big clock finished booming, while close by a church bell picked up the chimes; but when they died away it was very quiet again. There was no sign of life in the courtyard back of the Ca' Vespucci except a dim lamp burning under the archway, a whisper of music from one lighted window under the eaves, and a prowling cat flaring green eyes at d'Espinal out of the darkness.

The staff entrance was a studded door with a grilled peephole, and as d'Espinal approached it swung open silently, with the woman, Maria Spoletti he assumed, apparently waiting for him; she said, 'You are the picture expert?' It was like something out of a Venetian melodrama by Goldoni; and with the ripe figure and full lips, the calculating appraisal in her eyes, she might well have been one of Goldoni's wenches herself. 'You will be very quiet,' she told him.

They went along a flagged passage, past a doorway on the left into what looked like a porter's vestibule, and another heavy door on the other side. At the end were two more, one again to the right and the other facing them, and she opened this to reveal a flight of stone steps and an iron handrail let into the wall. These led up to a corridor running right and left, still in stone but noticeably warmer; the service steps and passages to the first floor, d'Espinal calculated, the reception floor. Here Maria turned left again and up yet more steps to a final door; padded with leather on this side but, when she drew it back, disguised with elegant ivory and gilded panelling on the other.

This corridor was thickly carpeted, brocaded chairs placed against the walls, pictures which d'Espinal suspected had originally come from Paolo's gallery, and under the window at the end a carved and gilt console table with a great bowl of flowers. Like a conventional guide Maria announced, 'We are now in the private apartments; you will please to be very careful,' and opened one more door.

He looked round incredulously at the crowded room, the two paintings after Landseer, the old desk and the cocktail cabinet, and then glanced back at Maria. She was watching him, and she said expressionlessly, 'That is what you have come to look at,' and nodded at the blank wall with the dull green drapes and strange half religious appearance. 'There is one thing,' she added. 'You must not touch it. Our butler and the cook and two of the men are all in the house; if you touch that picture, even with a finger, I promise you they will arrive here in a few seconds. And the police in a minute more.'

D'Espinal nodded briefly. 'Alarms? Very well. Now let me see it.'

Maria reached out to the white cord; the strip light came on as the curtains slid apart, and the portrait glowed out suddenly in its soft, idealized style. For a time, which afterwards he felt must have lasted for hours, d'Espinal was quite still; frozen with a recognition, an intuitive knowledge which did not need experts and all the paraphernalia of science to prove. He knew with absolute certainty that this was undoubtedly the most beautiful Botticelli he had ever seen. Simonetta Vespucci looked out at him with her faint half smile; and he knew in a moment of awful self realization that he wanted that picture for himself as he had never wanted anything before—and there was almost nothing he would not do to get it. Half like a prayer he whispered, 'Dear God; dear Loving God.'

Maria snapped, 'Be careful!' and he jerked back, as if awakening suddenly, still staring at the picture.

He could have studied it for hours; that permanently golden afternoon in the background, the flowing detail of the hair, the modelling of the face. As it was he contented himself with the condition of the paint and then, feeling that Maria was becoming impatient, murmured, 'Yes; a pretty thing. One cannot be certain of course.'

'Certain of what?' she demanded.

D'Espinal looked at her coldly. 'That it is a Botticelli. For the moment I would not care to pronounce. You may cover it up again.' Maria eyed him doubtfully but drew the curtains back and he added, 'We need its history; we have to know where it came from. Without that...' He shook his head. 'I must not waste any more of your time.'

'I do not understand,' Maria started. 'Miss Pentecost...'

'Miss Pentecost does not realize.' He smiled at her and went on, 'There is only one possibility. The young person who is staying here; she is at work on that history, is she not?' Maria's eyes veiled suddenly and he asked, 'Has she yet revealed anything?'

Maria did not answer and d'Espinal idly opened the leather case on its table beneath the picture. The sudden flare of the apparent emeralds startled him momentarily until he realized they were only replicas, but when he glanced back at Maria—as he told Paolo afterwards—the sheer cupidity in her eyes was as green as those glass beads themselves. 'So?' he breathed to himself, and said, 'There you have it, signorina. There is a doubt. But if the young lady were to make some useful discovery. And if I were to be informed of it...'

'That may not be possible.'

'I fear it must be.' D'Espinal's voice sharpened suddenly. 'Tell me, signorina, precisely what part does that young woman have in this enterprise?'

Maria stiffened for a moment and then shrugged.

'That is Miss Pentecost's affair. And you have now been here too long; it would be serious if you were seen.'

She turned abruptly and he followed her obediently through the panelled opening, down the service steps and passages; a route he considered he could remember sufficiently well should the need arise. Neither of them spoke until they reached the outer door but then d'Espinal said softly, 'There is one other person, signorina. A rascally looking fellow with two fingers lost from one hand. One, Giacomo Vespe.'

Reaching out to the heavy bolts on the door Maria stopped short, looking up at d'Espinal with her eyes glittering in the dull yellow light. It was several seconds before she said, 'I do not know of him. Who is he?'

'A rough, uncouth rascal. A type, one feels, who might well be engaged to arrange for, or even to remove, some slight inconvenience.'

'I do not know of him,' Maria repeated. She added urgently, 'Will you please to go at once.'

'Most unwillingly,' d'Espinal murmured. 'But I dare to hope that we shall meet again.'

CHAPTER SEVEN

Simone swore softly, pushing her fingers through her hair. She muttered, 'I might've known, Arturo. I might have guessed you wouldn't make it as simple as that.'

By next morning she had made up a table of the Etruscan characters and their modern equivalents. She had discovered too that when you got the knack of them they were surprisingly easy to remember and to write; but there she had come to a dead end. She had started hopefully on Arturo's manuscript with her customary feeling of excitement; and, before she reached the end of the first sentence she had realized with blank certainty that she was still no nearer to the answer.

In fact, she thought, scowling at her half dozen or so attempts, on the whole the original Etruscan looked more rational than the transcription. Some of those symbols indeed were vaguely recognizable as modern characters; yet what it came out to was not only meaningless but also apparently devoid of any rational pattern or rhythm. Arturo Vespucci's cipher manuscript now started, "Tz gczlti pi oluildfzdi lsfo pi tsuoei to eufobsfs..."

'Like all the monkeys in the universe banging on all the typewriters in the universe,' Simone said, 'and not writing Hamlet.'

Studying the few lines of script she told herself

that a professional cryptographer would probably break it in minutes and a computer, fed with the letter frequencies, in seconds; but she had little more than a vague general idea of either process. It had to be fairly simple since Arturo seemed to have written it quite fluently; and it was almost certainly some form of substitution—and therefore open to experiment. But she might make dozens, if not hundreds, of trials before stumbling on to the correct combination. That could only be a last hope after every other logical approach had failed.

She had already noticed that where he quoted dates Arturo had continued to use standard modern figures. At first this had looked careless until she realized that Etruscan or Roman numerals would have been too cumbersome to use, while—as she discovered for herself—it was in fact extraordinarily difficult to invent nine completely new characters, all quite distinct from the ancient letters and from each other. Then what had appeared to be an uncharacteristic slip for Arturo to make suddenly became the possibility of another lead. What she needed was two or more dates relating to known events or people. There was a chance then that she might recognize some pattern of letters near them; Simonetta, for instance, should be fairly clear, or perhaps Medici or Botticelli.

In the end she found half a dozen or so; and the first was 1944. But neither that nor any of the others seemed to offer any clue. It was only when she came to the last one, in the pages apparently written after Arturo's final return to Venice with the picture, that the answer appeared. This was 1478; two years after the death of Simonetta herself. The year of the

Pazzi Conspiracy, said to have been planned by Pope Sixtus IV for the destruction of the Medici power, when Giuliano de' Medici was assassinated in Florence Cathedral during High Mass, one of the most shocking murders in history.

Simone put down the date on a clean page of her note book and began doggedly to transcribe the last few groups of Etruscan characters leading up to it. At first sight they looked no more promising than any of the others; indeed they seemed even more ludicrous, reading "...qocnozli rc zeezee lsnnz hzaao uieh tso 1478...." She muttered, 'Quocknozli rc Zeezee; it sounds like an Aztec pop singer,' but then jammed her glasses more firmly on her nose in sudden excitement and stared at the words again.

That date had either to mean the Pazzi Conspiracy or the murder of Giuliano, perhaps both; there was nothing else to which it could refer. And "Pazzi" had the peculiarity of containing the first and last letters of the alphabet in a very simple construction. Arturo, in spite of his inveterate habit of contraction, would scarcely try to abbreviate that; he would leave it in five letters—which could be the group "Hzaao". The word "Murder" would have to be based on the Italian "Assassinare", and he would typically shorten that to "Assass". So it became possible that "Assass" was "Zeezee"; if it was that might make the "Z" of the "Hzaao" group into "A", and logically, therefore, "A" would be represented by "Z". Arturo had simply transposed the entire alphabet, using it backwards against the Etruscan equivalents.

Making a key of the Etruscan characters against the modern alphabet Simone started again, and this time the opening sentence came out easily. Apparently written here in Venice Arturo said, "After meeting Neri have decided to put all further notes in cipher", and then went on, "Did not expect any of this to be mixed up with the war". It all started simply enough, he wrote. Almost as he was preparing to leave for home, discouraged and tired, he received a message at his hotel asking him to telephone a Signor Neri in Fiésole. Not particularly interested by then, he did so largely as a matter of courtesy. But fifteen minutes later he was driving out fast to the village in the hills.

It appeared that Neri, now retired, had at one time been an art dealer. He still had his connections in Florence, and through them he had heard that Mr Vespucci had been making enquiries as to the possible existence of a certain picture. He had considered this for some days and had now decided that it might be advisable to meet Mr Vespucci; the name in itself, he said, was arresting. Signor Neri then gave Arturo an excellent lunch and subjected him to an intensive examination on his interests and his intentions.

Apparently Arturo satisfied him because Signor Neri proceeded to explain cautiously that there was a picture, or there had been a picture, as recently as October 1944; and, although he would not care to say it was the one in which Mr Vespucci was interested, there was a possibility that it might be. At that time, he said, the German armies were preparing a final stand on a line only a few miles to the east and running north of Florence; in particular hinged on a village called Pieve San Stefano. He did not profess to understand the military details, having always regarded the whole war as an intolerable interruption of civilized life; and in any case they did not matter.

What was important was that he had a very dear, although rather younger, friend and distant relative who was some kind of under officer—he was vague about this too—of the German army near San Stefano. This Paul Meisner was not only a brave and excellent man, he was also an expert, although an amateur, on Italian Renaissance painting. And in the early days of October that year Signor Neri had received a letter from Paul Meisner by the hand of a young countryman; one of those boys who appeared to make a nightly habit of passing to and fro through the fighting lines about some, no doubt, suspicious business of their own. This letter he would place in Mr Vespucci's hands on receiving certain assurances from him, but for the present it would be enough to give him merely the gist of it, together with certain other information which he had contrived to acquire subsequently.

Written secretly and in danger it had been difficult to read. But in effect it said that Paul Meisner had discovered certain items of incalculable artistic and historical value which must not fall into the hands of any of the armies; German, British or American. They had been secreted in a remote religious house, the Convent of the Holy Crown near the mountain village Caprese Michelangelo, for many hundreds of years; where the sisters not only did not appear to realize what they were but also somewhat disapproved of them.

How Meisner discovered this, how the sisters came to trust him so completely, Signor Neri did not know; he thought it probably never would be known. But somehow, presumably by his own integrity, the German officer had persuaded them that these treasures must be taken to a place of safety. And he himself arranged secretly for them to be brought to Florence by one of these sisters, with an adventurous local boy as her guide.

Simone thought of Arturo writing to Frau Meisner—wondering also when they themselves would hear from her, whether she too was dead—and Arturo himself broke off to comment, "What a man this Meisner must have been; he'd know what would happen to him if some of his own authorities discovered what he was doing".

The sister never arrived. Only the boy, Bruno, appeared; exhausted, a bullet scratch in his arm, half hysterical with shock and terror. Neri took him in, looked after him for some weeks, and slowly pieced together what had happened. According to Bruno the people of that area now were less afraid of the soldiers on both sides than they were of the partisan bands, who appeared often to be fighting a private war of their own. He and Sister Ursula—who was known as 'The Little Bear' both because of her name and her gruff uncompromising manner—got away from the convent easily enough that night and worked out into the hills; but just after crossing the Bibbiena road they blundered into a partisan group in the woods. And one of them he recognized; a local commander named Vespe, known as 'The Wasp'.

It was then, in the light of the partisans' torches, that Bruno saw for the first time what he and Sister Ursula were taking away between them. Wrapped separately in canvas there was a picture of a lady, a green necklace in a wooden box, and a golden book; and when the men asked what these were Sister Ursula said that long ago they had come to the convent with a great person named Vespucci. On this the man Vespe announced that he and his group would take these over in the name of the new Italian State; but even then all might have been well otherwise had not Sister Ursula, true to her character, started to abuse all of them.

For a minute or two apparently the scene had an almost comic turn before it plunged suddenly into tragedy. The partisans began teasing Sister Ursula; one of them snatched disrespectfully at her habit, and she retaliated by beating him over the head with the heavy stick she was carrying. And Vespe, holding a Sten gun, although he had two fingers missing on his left hand, quite simply shot her. Apparently that froze even Vespe's men. For a few seconds again, while the sky flickered and artillery hammered ominously not far away, they all stood staring down at the nun. One of them, Bruno remembered, crossed himself; and then Bruno himself bolted. Someone fired after him and he felt a bullet snatch at his shoulder, but he went on running. In the end he found a hole under the trees somewhere, crawled into it and lay there all the next day.

After this Signor Neri, as he said, had not known which way to turn. During that autumn and the bitter winter which followed the confusion became such that nobody knew what was happening anywhere, and he had decided there was nothing he could do. For a year or so he had heard rumours of the man Vespe but since then nothing; although Bruno was still to be found, married and now living in Arezzo, he thought. Finally he asked only an assurance from Mr Vespucci that in the event of finding the picture he would restore it to its rightful place; and also that he would then make known the entire story in the hope that some kind of justice might yet be done. He said, "Many of these partisans were fine enough fellows I believe; but this one was a murderer."

Simone was still staring at that when Becky came in, followed by Maria. Becky scolded, 'Don't forget you've got a fitting at Donnabella's, Simone,' and then demanded, 'Lord love us, girl, whatever's the matter? You look as if you've seen a ghost.'

'I rather feel as if I have,' Simone said. 'And I'm beginning to think you're right about that picture, too; it's dangerous.' She went on slowly, 'I've found Arturo's man with two fingers missing from his left hand.'

Maria caught her breath so sharply that Simone heard it and turned to look at her. The maid's face was strained and hard, but she lowered her eyes and murmured, 'Pardon me, principessa, signorina; if we do not go now we shall be late,' while Simone watched her for a second more before starting carefully to gather up all the papers and lock them back in the filing cabinet.

As its motor stopped and his boat drifted in towards the landing steps of Isola San Giorgio, d'Espinal viewed with considerable approval the four-storey tower against its sheltering cypress trees, the low pink house and the graceful arches and pergolas and glowing garden. 'A demi-paradise,' he murmured. 'A home of peace and, one might think, all the virtues.' When he stepped ashore Miss Pentecost, wearing a cool white dress, was lying in a long chair on the patio but she got up slowly and came across the grass to meet him. She said, 'It's nice of you to come.'

'Let me be plain, madame,' he told her, 'at the cost of some discourtesy. I am here only because it suits me. Otherwise I object to being bidden.'

'Bidden? But I invited you. Surely there's a difference? It's so convenient this afternoon. Aunt Judith's away visiting, on San Erasmo.' As they walked back towards the shade of the vines and the terra cotta jars overflowing with flowers, she went on, 'I wanted to see you again.'

'I imagine to explain the details of the ... operation?'

'Not exactly. I wanted someone to talk to; from outside.' She took a cigarette from the box on the table and lit it with curious, precise care. 'A few days ago you told me that I was a beautiful woman. I've been thinking about that.'

D'Espinal's eyes opened a fraction wider. 'I remember the occasion. I also said beware lest you fall into error.'

She sat down and a pretty little maid came out carrying a tray with elegant and gracious china on it. Miss Pentecost smiled, 'Thank you, Graziella,' and asked, 'Milk or lemon?' When the girl left she said, 'I had a feeling that I wanted to explain myself. Can you imagine what it's like being on this island weeks and months and years? Nothing to do but stare at Venice every night. From here it looks like a string of glass beads on the water.'

'Many people might envy you. You're merely saying that Satan finds mischief for idle hands.'

Miss Pentecost laughed suddenly. 'You're quite a moralist. I hear you've seen the Botticelli.'

'I've seen a picture,' he answered expressionlessly, 'which might perhaps be a Botticelli.'

She said, 'You've seen a Botticelli. You know that as well as I do. You know that one can't mistake the real thing. It's a sort of recognition; something almost physical.'

'Now,' he enquired softly, 'how do you understand that curious fact, Miss Pentecost?'

'Is it so curious? I was a painter myself at one time; not a very good one. A painter with all the technique but no creativeness; I was a copyist.' D'Espinal said nothing, and she went on, 'Mostly in the Louvre. I used to specialize in copies of The Mystic Marriage of St Catherine; the Correggio. You'll find that very funny.'

'I find it excruciating.'

'And the Mona Lisa, of course. She was always a good selling line. I can't tell you how much I got to hate that simpering, sexless bitch. Did you ever know a painter named Hugo?'

'I've seen a little of his work. It's poor stuff.'

'I always thought so. I was his mistress then; quite intense while it lasted. Until he introduced me to the next candidate; and then he told me that if ever I gave birth it would be another reproduction of the Mona Lisa already in a gold frame. I suppose I ran away, coming here...' She stopped and looked slightly surprised. 'I don't often talk about this.'

'You flatter me by so doing.' And it might even

be useful to know a little more about the ladies of San Giorgio, d'Espinal thought. He asked, 'And Mrs Teestock?'

'Judith? She was in Paris at that time and she insisted on bringing me back here. I think she felt she was saving me; but it was just after her own husband died and she was very much alone herself. I'm very fond of her, you know; and grateful,' Miss Pentecost added defensively. 'I really am. But I sometimes think she should have been the Mother Superior of a convent. That's her real vocation.'

The conception of the Mother Superior of a convent engaged about what was probably to be one of the most audacious art thefts in history struck d'Espinal as having a sort of harlequinade improbability, but he asked, 'While you, I imagine, find life here somewhat constricting?'

Miss Pentecost caught the dry tone in his voice and flushed. 'I ought not to bore you with these personal details.'

'Not that,' he said gravely. 'Whatever you might do, Miss Pentecost, it could never be that.' He brooded for a minute and then suggested, 'Shall we return to our immediate affair? In short, how d'you plan to bring this business off? You tell me you're a copyist. So I assume you've made a duplicate of the portrait?' She nodded, and he went on heavily, 'In that case I must tell you; however good it may be it will not deceive an expert for five minutes.'

Back to her normal manner Miss Pentecost smiled at him. 'Like your little Correggio?' He stared at her wickedly and she said, 'I'm sorry. I must learn not to offend you. My copy's not intended to deceive anyone. If you replace one picture which everybody believes to be a forgery with another which really is, who knows? Or cares?'

He murmured softly, 'One had thought it must be something like that. And how do you effect the substitution?'

'That's been rather carefully organized. It hangs on two small keys. One cuts off the alarm; the other opens the safe.'

'Why the safe?'

Watching her through half closed eyes he saw Miss Pentecost hesitate before she said, 'The real emeralds are in there.'

'And they are Maria Spoletti's perquisite?'

'Yes. It suits us. Obviously you can't have genuine emeralds left against a forged picture. That certainly would look odd.'

'I take the point. If one thing is true the other might have been.' But there was more to it than that, he thought; Miss Pentecost appeared to be oddly evasive. He asked, 'Does Maria realize how little those jewels are worth? Renaissance emeralds would come from Egypt; of that size they will be poor quality, dull and flawed. There is some heavy gold with them, but not enough to tempt any truly dedicated thief.'

Miss Pentecost shrugged. 'That's her affair. In any case she expects a quarter of what the picture fetches.'

'If we sell the picture,' d'Espinal reminded her gently.

He was certain that Miss Pentecost did not want to talk about the safe. She said, 'The keys are at Becky Kodaly's bank. They've been there ever since Arturo Vespucci died; and Becky can only get them by giving twenty-four hours' notice in writing, receiving them from the manager personally, and signing a receipt for them.'

'And how often does she do that?'

'She hasn't done it ever; yet.'

'Then why now?'

'That's what we had to arrange. On the nineteenth, which is Becky's birthday, she's giving a party. She's going to show the picture for the first time and present Miss Greenwood; as an historical expert, and perhaps even as a descendant of the Vespucci.'

'There's already a story to that effect going round.'

'Is there?' Miss Pentecost watched a boat with a painted sail sliding past over the blue water. 'It's wonderful the way it's all fitted together; almost as if it were intended. We've been thinking about it for years, Judith and I; working it out like some kind of puzzle game. Judith's clever at that sort of thing.'

'Pray let us continue,' d'Espinal suggested. 'The princess gives a party and exhibits the portrait. Which apparently necessitates procuring the alarm keys from her bank. Why?'

'Becky can't show the picture in her stuffy little sitting-room. It'll have to be moved down to the big reception salon on the first floor; which means cutting off the alarm first.'

'And then?'

Miss Pentecost said calmly, 'You'll change the picture for my copy, before the reception.'

'I...?' D'Espinal's eyes jerked open. 'I beg your pardon. Did I hear you correctly? I shall?'

'Of course; that's your part. The salon will be locked up; there'll be no one there for two hours before the reception and Maria will let you in and out by the service stairs. It's all arranged.'

'Superb,' d'Espinal breathed. 'Masterly, madame. And after this delightful exercise?'

'That doesn't matter for you. You'll be on the night train for Milan by then. But as we see it Professor Venturi will look at the portrait first; Becky's invited him specially for that. And he'll say at once that it's a forgery. Then of course there'll be a certain amount of confusion.'

'There probably will,' d'Espinal agreed solemnly. 'It might even become noticeable. And the emeralds?'

Miss Pentecost hesitated again. 'I said there'll be some confusion. The emeralds are Maria's affair, but one imagines they'll get lost. Then afterwards the imitation set will be found somewhere; on the floor perhaps. It's all so simple,' she finished. 'A copyist Botticelli and glass emeralds. Everybody will say that poor Becky's been deluding herself for years. And no doubt Mrs Medina-Silvestro will give tongue. There's one thing certain; nobody will believe there was ever a real picture or real jewels.'

D'Espinal said, 'You fascinate me, Miss Pentecost.' He closed his eyes, thinking for a time of the sheer devilment of the plan.

Miss Pentecost was defensive again. 'It was Becky herself who started it; being so foolish. When she married Stefan Kodaly Judith was terribly shocked. She considered it was almost indecent; and it was quite clear that he was after the picture himself. Judith was beginning to get worried about money at that time, and I remember her saying "When I think of all the good we might do with these things". That was the germ of the idea; and it grew into wondering if we really could do it. And then into working out how.'

'And your present stratagem?'

'That was Becky again. She came across a photograph and a ridiculous article about Greenwood in some women's magazine. You can't imagine what it did to her. She actually convinced herself it was some kind of message from Arturo. She had to meet this girl, she had to have her out here. We did try to stop her. We told her if Miss Greenwood was the sort of person to make impossible claims about her descent there was no telling what else she might do. But that made Becky more obstinate still. And then we began to see how we could use her. In the end Judith said it might just as well be a sign to us that we were meant to take those things and do something useful with them.'

'I perceive,' d'Espinal murmured, 'that Mrs Teestock truly believes the Lord works in wondrous ways.'

'It was certainly providential, this girl turning up. Without her Becky would never have dreamed of giving a party and showing the picture. But when she got so excited, persuading herself that magazine article was a "sign" from Arturo, it was quite easy to put the idea into her mind through Maria. Maria's very clever at suggesting things to Becky and letting her imagine that she thought of them herself.'

D'Espinal watched Miss Pentecost with something like admiration in his half-closed eyes. 'Tell me about Stefan Kodaly.'

'He was just a confidence trickster, though he really did have some kind of charm. And I always thought he was good for Becky; when he came along she was getting very peculiar. He made her go around; buy clothes again. And he cleared all of the old servants out of the Ca' Vespucci and brought a complete new staff in.'

'Including Maria?'

Miss Pentecost smiled faintly. 'Maria was his mistress. She's an odd person. She despises poor Becky. But that still doesn't prevent her being an almost perfect ladies' maid.'

'Where did Kodaly come from?'

'Does it matter? I heard something about Zurich. When he appeared in Venice he was living on the Via Garibaldi.'

'The Via Garibaldi?' d'Espinal repeated. 'A somewhat doubtful district for a prince.'

'He was a somewhat doubtful prince.'

'The Via Garibaldi reminds me.' Watching Miss Pentecost carefully he asked, 'Do you know anything of a man named Vespe? Giacomo Vespe? A fellow of no charm at all with two fingers missing from his left hand.'

Miss Pentecost looked puzzled. 'Ought I to? Because I don't. Why?'

There was no doubt she was telling the truth, and he explained, 'An idle question, I hope. But one hears gossip that he is known to Maria. A friend of hers, do you think?'

'Gossip?' Miss Pentecost laughed. 'I'm starting to understand why you came to Venice a week early. It's probably quite simple. Maria's man mad, but too careful to indulge herself at the Ca' Vespucci. There's nothing in that. I don't imagine she's talkative in bed.'

'Let us hope she is not.' D'Espinal brooded on

that for a moment, thinking that he would have expected Maria to look for a more lovesome bedfellow, and then asked, 'May one see your copy of the portrait? I confess to an impatient interest.'

'Why not?' Miss Pentecost said. She got up and led him along the house, through dappled sunlight under the pergola to the foot of the tower. Inside there was a wine press and casks, the husbandry tools of an Italian country house, and a flight of steps. They went up these and past two landings to a heavy door high up under the old rafters fitted with a new Yale lock, and Miss Pentecost took the key from her handbag to open it into a wide light room with an aromatic scent of paint and oil and tempera. There was an easel with a panel on it under a drape, one big table littered with tubes of paint and pots and brushes and another covered with photographs. It was professional and efficient; Miss Pentecost, d'Espinal thought, was clearly no amateur.

Without hesitation she swung the easel round and took away the cloth. Once more the face of Simonetta Vespucci looked out at d'Espinal and he gazed back at it nodding gently, trying to hide his surprise; a real admiration of Miss Pentecost's totally unexpected ability. There was, indeed, very little immediately discernible difference from the original. The colour was perhaps a thought colder, although he was not quite sure even of that, the manner fluent, and somehow she had even contrived to give it the gentle bloom of age which so beautifully softened the real picture; it was again a permanently golden afternoon. One could not expect it to deceive an expert for a minute, he told himself firmly; but one had to admit that for most other people ...

'Well?' she asked.

'Well,' he repeated. 'I will be round with you, madame; most excellently well. Always you surprise me afresh.'

She said, 'I even studied the methods of van Meegeren; the Vermeer forger. The panel's not right but it's near enough. Of course the colour chemistry's impossible and the paint's nothing like as hard as it should be. It won't stand examination.' She laughed a little breathlessly. 'But it doesn't have to. Don't you think,' she asked slowly, 'that between us we might make ... quite a partnership?'

D'Espinal stared back at her blankly over his shoulder. 'I beg you, madame,' he protested, 'let us conclude one affair before we speculate on others. How the devil did you do this?'

'It was the first step, whatever we planned, to make a copy. For more than a year Judith had Becky over here at least once a week, while I went to the Ca' Vespucci; studying the original and taking photographs.' She nodded to the colour prints which littered one of the tables. But at that moment they heard the stutter of a boat from below and Miss Pentecost went to the window to look down. She announced, 'Judith's back,' and turned to face d'Espinal again. 'There's only one thing.' There was a sudden surprising hint of anger in her voice. 'The trouble is that Judith wants to cry off now. We've gone so far and she wants to give up. Tell me,' she asked, 'quite definitely. Do you want that picture?'

'Quite definitely,' d'Espinal answered, 'I intend to have it.'

They listened to the boat and the sound of voices; Pietro and Mrs Teestock. 'In that case,' Miss Pentecost told him, 'you've got to be careful with her; she could easily spoil everything. You've got to tell her that nothing can possibly go wrong. Judith's weak, that's her trouble. "Letting 'I dare not' wait upon 'I would'",' she quoted. '"Like the poor cat i' the adage".'

D'Espinal looked at her from under his eyelids. 'I find that peculiarly apposite,' he murmured. 'Not the quotation, perhaps, so much as yourself as Lady Macbeth, Miss Pentecost. Let us go down then. You shall present me to the lady, and I will endeavour to be at my most persuasive.'

CHAPTER EIGHT

Becky sat patiently at the big desk while Simone turned over her notes; looking ridiculously young again, the old lady thought, with her heavy glasses and her air of absorbed efficiency. She still could not quite get over the idea of a girl as pretty as this, and as charming when she chose, being so professional and determined. Arthur would have taken to her, he'd have recognized her as another of his own kind; and there was no doubt that he would have agreed wholeheartedly with what she, Becky, had in mind to do about the child.

'It's clear enough now,' Simone was saying. 'Arturo met Signor Neri several times again before Neri died in 1961.'

'That's another one,' Becky murmured.

'He was an old man too,' Simone answered. 'Then Arturo spent July and September that year tracing Bruno Longhi and the surviving members of Vespe's partisan group. Apparently Bruno was still frightened; he wanted to talk mostly about the artillery fire and as he put it, the sky going up and down. That made an extraordinary impression on his mind. But in the end he gave a dreadful description of Vespe shooting Sister Ursula. I think he probably embroidered it.'

'Would it need any embroidering?'

'I shouldn't have thought so. But at last he gave Arturo the name of a man who now kept a bar in Arezzo. Bruno refused to have anything to do with it and Arturo went to this bar alone. He says the man who kept it was a pig, and he refused to talk. But one of the customers followed Arturo out, took him somewhere which he said was safer, and gave him several more names. Arturo says he thought it was a matter of paying off an old score against Vespe or his people. For more than a week after that he scoured the countryside round Arezzo finding the rest of the group; and eventually he was put on to another man, now working as a stone mason, at a place called Citta di Castello. This one had been Vespe's second in command, and they said that he'd always been more than prepared to shoot Vespe himself; if he could ever have got behind him to do it. Arturo says, "Another pig; but this time a pig who takes money", and he told Arturo where to find Vespe; at San Sepolcro. It's an ancient little walled town in the Upper Tiber Valley; and not far from Pieve San Stefano.'

'Where they murdered the sister...' Becky stared across the room at Paul Meisner's picture of the Ponte Vecchio and muttered rather peevishly, 'All that and Arthur never told me a word.'

'I think he felt it was too risky.' Simone carefully did not mention one note; "The less Becky knows about this the better; she opens her mouth too much sometimes, and I don't want anybody else to come looking for this picture. And it could be dangerous..." Simone said, 'I'm only here because Arturo didn't talk about it.'

'There is that,' Becky agreed. 'The Lord don't hurry Himself,' she added obscurely. 'Go on, child.'

'That was in July. But when Arturo got to San Sepolcro he couldn't find Vespe. And he was tired.'

'He got home downright exhausted; and obstinate with it. I was vexed with him; as any woman would be.'

Arturo had mentioned that too; it was another note which might best be forgotten, Simone thought. She went on, 'In September he came back and searched the whole district again. Incidentally he found that they'd rebuilt the Convent. He still didn't locate Vespe, but he became quite certain that there were people who knew where he was. And then he says that you wrote and insisted on his returning to Venice. You went to Cannes for the winter and then on to America.'

'I was getting afraid for him,' Becky said rather defensively. 'He was driving himself to death.'

'So it was June of 1962 before he got back to San Sepolcro again. And this time he discovered that Vespe really was there. He was living and working on one of the remote hill farms with his widowed sister; up near a place called Monte Casale.' Simone paused, and then finished, 'There's something very curious here, Becky. The sister's name was Spoletti.'

Becky stared for a moment before sitting up sharply and asking, 'Eh?'

'The name was Spoletti.'

'D'you mean to suggest that Maria...? It's a coincidence, love. It must be.'

'I'm not suggesting anything,' Simone answered precisely, 'only giving you the facts. It's not an uncommon name and it doesn't prove anything.'

'All the same,' Becky muttered, 'it's funny.'

'I think so too. Has she ever given you cause to be suspicious.'

Becky considered that. 'Nothing you could ever

put your finger on. Perhaps we'd best let it be. Go on, love.'

Simone turned back to her notes. 'Vespe. He's the man Arturo told you about; the man with two fingers missing from his left hand.' Becky whispered sharply, 'That one!' and Simone went on, 'Arturo says, "They call him the Wasp. He's a natural bully; give him a weapon and he's a killer. And stupid." All the same it took Arturo nearly two weeks to get him to admit that he did have the Vespucci relics. Because Vespe was afraid himself.'

'He'd have good cause to be.'

'It rather looks like it. Arturo used threats, blackmail and money and eventually he goaded Vespe into breaking down; partly because Vespe always had the idea of selling those things anyway. The trouble was that he didn't know how. There was the portrait and the necklace. And a breviary, or a Book of Hours. Arturo describes that as unbelievable.'

'And bad luck with it,' Becky mumbled. 'Worse than the picture. I don't even like to talk about that thing.'

'"A gold cover worked in high relief and decorated with inset emeralds and pearls,"' Simone read. '"Written on vellum and illustrated with twelve miniatures; allegories of the style of Primavera and The Birth of Venus, undoubtedly by Botticelli himself."' She took off her glasses to look at Becky. 'That's why Arturo was so interested in The Very Rich Hours of the Duc de Berry in the Musée Condé.' Putting them on again she continued, '"Containing an inscription, probably in Giuliano's own hand, to the effect that it was made for Giuliano de' Medici and presented to his Queen of Love, Simonetta Vespucci, in 1476."'

'That night Arthur came back,' Becky muttered, 'near enough finished up himself, he reckoned it'd be the last thing the poor girl had in her hands when she died. And if you ask me there's been death on it ever since.'

'I don't know about that,' Simone murmured, 'but it must be one of the biggest art discoveries ever.' She stopped and for a few seconds the bare, cool room was very quiet before she went on factually, 'In the end Arturo argued Vespe into taking a hundred and fifty thousand American dollars; which seemed to have amused Arturo, made him more than ever convinced that Vespe was a fool. He spent the rest of the summer realizing that money very carefully and gradually so there shouldn't be any questions asked. By October he'd placed it to an account in Zurich. Finally he arranged for Vespe and the entire family to disappear from San Sepolcro overnight; Vespe didn't want any questions asked either if it got about that he'd suddenly come into a lot of money. And that's about all,' she finished. 'Except there is one more reason why Arturo didn't tell even you too much. Because legally he was a receiver of stolen property.'

'I always thought so. It's something we shall have to put right.' She looked at Simone uncertainly. 'I'll tell you straight, love; I like your company here and I want you to stay on. My Arthur was a great man and I want to see him put where he ought to be. So you've got a big book to write now. Will you do it for me?'

Simone hesitated. 'I'd like to. But I must tell you that some of his ideas are rather far out. And a lot of people are going to laugh at them.'

'Arthur wouldn't mind. What ideas?'

'Apart from finding the relics, historical theories. About Giuliano de' Medici's children; and how those things found their way to the Convent of the Holy Crown. Arturo never believed that Giuliano's love affair with Simonetta Vespucci was purely platonic. He thought that besides the illegitimate son who became Pope Clement VII—he was born in 1478, two years after Simonetta's death—Giuliano had an earlier child by Simonetta herself. A daughter who was adopted by the Vespucci and then much later entered the convent, taking her mother's treasures with her. He suggests that Simonetta might actually have died in giving birth to the child. I'm sorry, Becky, but it's really too fanciful, you know.'

'It could account for you,' Becky answered.

'That's more than improbable.' Rather impatiently Simone started gathering the papers together. 'I'd like to see the Book of Hours.'

'It's best where it is,' Becky said flatly. 'And I shall feel happier when it's out of this house for good.' She went on, 'There's just one more thing now; for my party. There'll be somebody here from the *Gazzettino*, that's the local newspaper. I want you to write out a little piece. About that convent and Sister Ursula, this Vespe and how my Arthur found the relics. What do they call it?'

'A press hand out.' Simone thought about that. 'Are you sure it's really wise? It's going to create quite a sensation.'

'That's what I'm counting on; and it's what my Arthur would have wanted. Maybe I'm a silly old woman, love, but I always thought there was death on those things and I'm sure of it now. They won't be safe until we've told the whole story and sent 'em back where they belong. And if we can set the police looking for that murdering villain at the same time so much the better. Now then,' she went on briskly, 'let's have done with it for today. We've got your fitting at Donnabella's and we shall have Miss Maria coming in to tell us so any minute. Maria Spoletti...' she repeated thoughtfully. 'I don't know what to make of that name.'

'Neither do I,' Simone admitted, conscious of a sudden slight uneasiness too formless to explain. 'There's another thing; also rather curious. Did you ever tell anyone, Miss Pentecost for instance, Arturo's theory that there could have been peculiar questions about Simonetta Vespucci's death?'

'Not that I know of,' Becky said. 'But I might've done. I remember Arthur used to talk about it sometimes in the early days; before he turned secretive. Why?'

Simone locked her papers into the filing cabinet carefully. 'Something she said in London; it's puzzled me quite a lot. I think I shall have to ask them; Miss Pentecost about that and Maria about her name.'

Becky cackled suddenly. 'You're a regular little detective. Ask them what you like, love; but not before the party, if you don't mind. I don't want Maria in one of her tantrums, she can be awkward when she chooses; and Emilia Pentecost's been very good in her managing way. You'll have plenty of time to clear everything up after my party.'

D'Espinal walked majestically under the shade

of the trees in the Gran Viale Santa Maria Elizabetta on the Lido, through the strolling chattering crowds and between bars and glittering shops, rows of tables and swinging seats and banks of flowers; children with their little dogs and monstrous beach toys, elegant ladies and hot sun-reddened ones, smart Milanese suits and open shirts and rumpled trousers. This time he had asked Miss Pentecost to meet him, and she had said four thirty at the café on the corner of the Via Scutari; a pleasant place from which one could still view the passing entertainment of this colourful, murmurous avenue. Nodding benevolently to the waiter he sat thinking, with some pleasurable anticipation, of the coming meeting. Miss Pentecost, he thought, appeared to manage Mrs Teestock with consummate skill, there was no doubt she considered she had a talent for management, and her ability as a forger showed almost infinite promise. Nevertheless it was time now to make their own relative positions quite unequivocally clear.

She was a few minutes late, but she came without any fluster. He liked that too; he could never tolerate self-excusing females. Sitting down and taking out a cigarette she said smilingly, 'Today it is I who am bidden.'

'Today,' he told her gravely, 'we have a little business to arrange. You're taking tea?' He waited until the waiter had served her and whisked away again and then continued, 'You will remember that a few days ago I mentioned certain of my associates; a small consortium, as it were?'

'Your associates in Paris?'

It did not particularly matter where she imagined

they were, but he nodded solemnly and went on, 'We have now concluded an agreement.' He paused impressively. 'I am authorised to offer you the sum of five hundred thousand pounds, to be deposited to your instructions on arrival of the object at any convenient point over the Italian frontier.'

Miss Pentecost chose a sliver of lemon, placed it in her teacup and asked, quite expressionlessly, 'Is that all?'

'Many people would regard it as a modest competence.'

She looked past him at the bright drifting crowds, smiling at a pretty small girl, before answering, 'We'd expected a great deal more. Maria wants a quarter of it. If I say it's not enough?'

In fact since the consortium was entirely fictional the figure was academic, but Miss Pentecost had to learn her place and he answered, 'In that case one would merely wish you good afternoon.'

'Aren't you forgetting your little Correggio and Tina Drikos?'

D'Espinal gazed at her reproachfully. 'Dear lady, that was an excellent joke while it lasted. It amused both of us. But now let me be quite clear; you are more in my power than I am in yours. A few words with this Princess Kodaly, or better still with Mrs Messina-Silvestro, would destroy your credit in Venice for ever.'

'They wouldn't believe you.'

'No?' D'Espinal leaned back in his chair. 'Your charming friend Miss Greenwood called on us the other day.'

That did startle Miss Pentecost. She put down her teacup with a sharp little clatter and demanded, 'She what? How does she know about you? And what did she want?'

'For the present,' he murmured, 'I will merely observe that Miss Greenwood is neither so trusting nor so naïve as you imagine ... In a word, to descend to the vernacular, I could now quite easily blow the whole thing.' He glanced from under his eyelids at Miss Pentecost and went on softly, 'Let us recognize our mutual interests.'

She laughed, suddenly and surprisingly. 'You're quite unique.'

'I have always thought so. We make a matching pair.'

'What did Greenwood say?'

'Does it matter?' he asked. 'Tell me instead the details, full and complete, of our whole operation tomorrow.'

She watched him for a moment and then said, 'Of course. I'd have told you on San Giorgio but you were so busy exerting your charm on Judith. She's quite taken by you.'

'And her fears are now somewhat allayed?'

'Completely so; she feels that nothing can possibly go wrong with you here.' D'Espinal closed his eyes complacently and Miss Pentecost laughed again. She started, 'In the morning Becky gets the keys from her bank; Judith and I go across in the afternoon to help with the final arrangements for the reception. I shall take my copy of the picture, in a case, and leave it in the old porter's lodge, just inside the staff entrance. And then some time between five and six, in her private apartments, Becky will switch off the alarms. The portrait will be taken down and carried to the reception salon on the first floor; it will be placed, behind curtains, on an easel in a big alcove near the orchestra rostrum. The main doors will then be locked and one of the footmen will be posted outside in the hall. We've gone to some trouble to suggest all this to Becky.'

'Admirable,' d'Espinal said. 'You plan a nefarious enterprise as to the manner born.'

'Becky will rest until eight o'clock when she will start to dress—with Maria, of course—and I shall keep Miss Greenwood in womanly chatter until it's time for us to dress too.' With his eyes closed d'Espinal nodded gently. 'By that time the entire staff, permanent and temporary, will be in the butler's parlour for their evening meal; and Maria will see to it that there's everything to keep them there. They'll be safe until eight thirty.'

'The house will be wrapped in peace; perfect. There are no detectives; policemen?'

'Only the man outside the salon. And we can send one of the waitresses to keep him amused. So; at half past seven you'll go to the staff entrance and Maria will let you in. You will pick up the copy, and she'll take you up the service passages to a door which opens directly into the alcove. You'll have nearly an hour and it should be quite simple to take the Botticelli out of its frame and put my copy in. You will then take it back to the porter's lodge. But for Heaven's sake be careful to keep to the right passage. That house is honeycombed with them and if you take the wrong one you might come out anywhere. They're a relic of the days when the wealthy Venetians considered that their servants should remain invisible.'

'It grows more Gothic every moment,' d'Espinal

breathed. 'After that I imagine my part in the frolic is over.'

'There's a train for Milan at nine forty. But I'd like you to wait in the lodge until half past eight. If you really want the history of the portrait.'

'The provenance? I shall need that, of course.'

'I should be able to let you have it by then. And I'd like to see you before you leave; to make the final arrangements.' D'Espinal studied her thoughtfully and she flushed. 'You force one to say things ... I want you to wait in Milan for me; I can meet you there in a few days.'

'Emilia,' he said softly, 'you think of everything. So be it; we shall meet in Milan.' Since he had no intention of going there in any case that was as academic as the five hundred thousand. 'And after I leave?' he asked. 'At the Ca' Vespucci?'

'The reception starts at nine. Then I shall slip away to get the replica emeralds from Becky's room, go through the service passages again, and change them for the real ones.'

'Why not Maria? The emeralds are her interest.'

'Maria will have the keys...' Miss Pentecost started involuntarily.

'The keys again,' d'Espinal said. 'What is it about these keys? Surely they'll have done their work by then?'

She hesitated and then went on quickly, 'Becky once told us that they look exactly like car ignition keys. And she's so short sighted and so absurdly vain that she won't wear her spectacles. So some time, perhaps while she's taking her bath, Maria will pick up the real ones and leave two others in their place. It doesn't matter.'

'I see,' d'Espinal murmured, as indeed he did. He had half suspected it before and he was certain now; there was something more in that safe, something which would never appear at the reception, perhaps the greatest prize of all. He thought of asking Miss Pentecost plainly, but dismissed the idea. It should not be too difficult to find out in his own good time and his own way; and if one could add both that and the emeralds to the portrait it should make a very fair collection. He suggested, 'Let us forget the keys then. But what if Miss Greenwood or the princess should check the picture before the reception?'

'They don't suspect anything; there's no reason why they should. And Maria will see to it that they won't have time. Not until ten o'clock when Becky makes her announcement and the curtains are drawn back. Professor Venturi will be the first to examine the portrait, and as you pointed out yourself he'll see through it immediately. After that one just doesn't know. Mrs Messina-Silvestro will leave, of course, and most of the others will go with her. They half expect the whole thing to be a farce anyhow. We shall stay behind to look after Becky.'

'She will call the police.'

'What can they do? Nobody in Venice has ever believed in that picture. They'll be soothing and sympathetic, but that will be the end of it. It will be the best thing for Becky, too; I promise you that. She'll close that house up and move away to Cannes; where she'll be really happy at last.'

'In short,' d'Espinal said, 'you conceive a crime with the most altruistic motives possible. It's a charming thought; the greatest good for all concerned. Except perhaps Miss Greenwood.'

Miss Pentecost's eyes narrowed. 'You should never have met that girl. I hope you're not going to get worried about her too.'

'I'm far from happy.' He brooded for a time and at last announced, 'Up to a point you may be right; there is little she can do. I have the feeling also that this Princess Kodaly's own title to the treasures could be doubtful; there is a strong smell of that about the whole affair. But have you ever thought seriously of the woman, Maria Spoletti? She is a bad one. You are merely bad in spots and streaks, as it were; there is the spark of a sudden and startling renaissance in you. It is part of your interest. But that woman is wicked all through. Have you ever seriously considered that, in the vulgar tongue, she may be planning to pull a fast one on you?'

'Often,' Miss Pentecost smiled. 'She's simply not clever enough.'

'Emilia,' he said heavily, 'be warned. That creature is clearly connected with a man who comes as near the ape as anything I have ever seen. And I do not believe the connection is simply an amiable frailty. The man's too old and too unprepossessing. There's devilment in it; and, I suspect, danger to the young woman, Greenwood.'

'You are getting worried,' Miss Pentecost accused him. 'D'you really think I'd have anything to do with that sort of thing? I'm not that bad, in spite of the spots and streaks. Even if I were we couldn't afford it. That really would set the police asking questions.'

'I hope Spoletti sees it that way,' he answered. 'For I must tell you, Emilia, even at the cost of sounding a little melodramatic, that I have never yet handled a picture with blood on it and I do not propose to start now. If anything touches that young woman I shall wash my hands of the whole business. And of you.' He was slightly surprised by his own fervour; even stopped for a second to wonder whether he really meant it.

'No, Harcourt,' Miss Pentecost said, 'I think on the whole I'd rather lose the picture. I promise you that from the moment we arrive at the Ca' Vespucci neither Judith nor I will let that girl out of our sight.'

Maria said, 'Every last word of it, Uncle 'Como.' She was facing Giacomo Vespe across the table under a single dim yellow light in the old porter's lodge. 'You're a fool. A fine bold soldier with a gun in your hand, when you shoot down a poor silly nun, but only a noisy dog without it.'

Vespe snarled at her and slapped the table top with his bare hand. 'It's forgotten now; all those years ago.'

'All those years,' she mocked. 'D'you think that changes it? Line by line, my brave uncle, that little signorina is writing your life away. Moreover she has now come upon the name Spoletti and sooner or later she will ask questions. I can lie, of course; but it is still dangerous.'

Vespe grunted, fumbled in his pocket, and tossed a box of the tiny wax vestas called cerini on to the table. 'So it's easy. You still have that key of Stefan's. Set light to these and drop them into Vespucci's damned papers.'

'Giacomo...' Maria stared at him pityingly. 'I cannot express what an idiot you are. Stefan always said you had no judgement. If we do that we might as clearly tell them in so many words that something is to happen. It must be arranged my way.'

'Very well then,' Giacomo said. 'There's water enough out there.'

'And when they find her; perhaps in a few days?' Maria asked. 'Don't you see there'll be yet more trouble? It must be something simpler, and safer. Come with me and I'll show you.' On one wall there was an old rack still hung with rows of big keys; she chose three of them deliberately saying, 'There is a place beyond the old wine cellar. Stefan found it. It was his plan to hide the treasures there for a time if we ever succeeded with them.'

She led the way out to the heavy door on the other side of the passage. Beyond it was a low vault, still with mouldering racks and a few dusty bottles, and a door again at the far end which in turn opened into a long narrow tunnel. There was an earthy stink and, as Maria flicked on a single dim globe, a glint of two red eyes and a whisper of movement, a glimpse of a scaly tail flicking away; but without hesitating she went on to fit the third key in a last and this time almost invisible door. It swung back ponderously on a stone chamber with neither window nor light and only a bare slab or ledge just raised above the floor level. Vespe stared into the small dark hole and then whispered, 'Holy Mother,' and edged back.

'That comes strangely from you,' Maria remarked. She added, 'It is said that in here they once found a skull with a leaden coronet nailed around it. No one could tell how long it had been there.' She shivered herself and went on defensively, 'I do not like it either; but I cannot think of any other way.'

Vespe turned back abruptly. He did not speak until they reached the service passage again, but then he grunted, 'You're a monster. No, Maria; I'm too old for that kind of work.'

'I do not like it myself,' she repeated. 'And you are by no means too old to spend the rest of your life in prison. Perhaps we may let her out in a day or two; if she swears to go away and say nothing. It will be a little discomfort; nothing more.'

Vespe thought that over slowly, blinking at her in the light. At last he muttered, 'If that's the way of it, very well. When do we do it?'

'You do it,' she corrected him sharply. 'I don't yet know when; it must be a little before the reception I think, but not too early. I'll warn you in time to be ready. Then I shall see to her baggage and those papers and afterwards swear that she left. So will the San Giorgio women; because they must.' She opened the door to the courtyard and held out the keys. 'You will need them.'

Vespe cursed bitterly and helplessly. 'It is Vespucci's doing, this; that swine. He swore he'd never write nor breathe one word.'

'You have always been too good and trustful, Uncle 'Como,' Maria said. 'It is your only weakness. Now go; and don't drink tonight. I shall obtain suitable clothes for you to wear, and you will present yourself at six o'clock tomorrow with the other extra men.'

She watched him cross the yard to disappear under the further archway, and then turned back to the house herself and went quietly in, closing and locking the big door with a curious air of absorbed finality.

CHAPTER NINE

Clipping one copy of the press announcement to her main notes Simone placed two more in a separate folder for the reception tonight. She still considered it was a mistake; that somewhere there was trouble in it. It was too sensational; and she more than suspected that the Italian newspapers would make the most of Bruno Longhi's description of the murder of Sister Ursula, they would drag everything they could out of the survivors of the partisan group. It only added horror to the Vespucci relics and, although she tried to dismiss the feeling because to her matter of fact mind it seemed to be as superstitious as Becky's own fancies, she could not shake off an obscure premonition that somehow the horror might perpetuate itself. 'And that's nonsense,' she told herself firmly, 'it's just that there really is an atmosphere about those things; and there is something odd about Pentecost and Maria. And tomorrow...'

She never finished the sentence. At that moment there was a light tap on the door and Alberto appeared murmuring diffidently, 'It is ten minutes gone seven, signorina, and Maria sends me to say your tray is taken up.' And damn Maria, Simone thought irritably, she was too officious by half and there were questions she would ask Maria tomorrow. But she had taken to Alberto by now; he was always around with a sort of shy devotion which flattered and amused her, made it impossible to be unkind to him, and she said, 'Very well, Alberto; I'm coming now.'

Locking the filing cabinet she took her folder with the press notes and followed him out and up to the main corridor, stopping there to look back at the hall. After the bustle of preparation all day the house now seemed very quiet; only two of the florists' girls putting the last touches to their flower decorations and a footman sitting importantly outside the closed doors to the salon. But there was another man coming out from the service passage at the foot of the stairs, a thick-set figure wearing ill-fitting waiter's dress clothes; he seemed startled by their appearance and moved aside quickly to disappear into one of the archways as they passed. It was curiously furtive, Simone thought, and in her sitting-room she asked, 'Should that man have been wandering about? I've never seen him here before.'

Alberto paused in setting out the table. 'It will be one of the extra staff. They send them from an agency, and some of them...' He shook his head disapprovingly. 'Not at all the correct type.' Opening the half bottle of Niersteiner—presumably another idea of Maria's—he ceremoniously poured a few drops for Simone to taste and enquired, 'Shall I serve the signorina?'

'You'll want to get your own meal,' she told him. 'It will be a long evening. Just bring my coffee and clear away later.'

It was twenty minutes to eight when he came back, almost time to start dressing, and Simone was standing at the window looking down at the canal below;

the awning out over the landing steps, and the men already waiting expectantly for the launches and gondolas which would crowd in later. She was half expecting Miss Pentecost, half hoping she would come, thinking that it could do no harm at least to talk carefully to her about Arturo Vespucci's ideas, and she took her coffee from Alberto and asked, 'Where is Miss Pentecost's room?'

He answered, 'She is on the floor above,' and added, 'That is a charming lady; always with a kind thought. Today when she came she gave me some fine postage stamps for my small nephew, who collects them.' He finished stacking the dishes on his tray and hesitated. 'If I might ask, signorina; a favour from you also. There was a very pretty one on your letter a few days since.'

Simone looked round at him sharply. 'On what?' she demanded.

'If I have said anything wrong...' he started. 'There was a letter from Germany.'

'But I've had no such letter,' she said. 'Where is it?'

He repeated, 'If I have said anything wrong ... I take in the mail each day, and I gave it to Maria; as I was instructed.'

'And who instructed you? Or can I guess? Where is she now? Maria?'

Never had Alberto imagined it was possible for this quiet signorina to put on such a different face. 'When I brought up your coffee, I saw her going into the old study; where the signorina has been working.' Simone moved across purposefully to the door and he said, 'Signorina, I am truly sorry.'

'You've nothing to be sorry about,' she told him

crisply. 'But Maria might have.'

The house was still very quiet, and the reception floor deserted except for the footman outside the salon; now sitting close to a young woman in the black and white dress of a waitress, with a bottle of wine and glasses on a tray beside them. One of the service panels was open too, letting in a cool draught and a faintly watery smell against the scent of the flowers everywhere; there Simone had a momentary impression of something in the shadows beyond it, but she went on without stopping down the short flight of private stairs to the study. Opening the door she paused, taking in both Maria and Miss Pentecost silhouetted against the fading greenish light from the window. They were standing at the open filing cabinet with her notes in their hands; reading the press hand-out.

For a second or two apparently they did not realize she was there, until Miss Pentecost jerked round suddenly, staring at Simone with her lips and eyes unnaturally dark against the pale face; then she whispered something, and Maria looked up too. None of them spoke, and in the silence Simone caught the sad call of a gondolier floating up from the canal below before hearing another movement behind her and glancing back to see Alberto inevitably outside. Closing the door on him, and oddly surprised by the flatness of her own voice, she asked, 'What exactly are you doing?'

The break gave Maria time to recover. Just as quietly she answered, 'It's unpardonable, this, signorina. But we came in here to look for you and found the cabinet open.'

'You're lying,' Simone told her levelly.

Miss Pentecost started to say something, but Maria cut in, 'If you please ... Signorina Greenwood has just said a very bad thing. She should explain.'

'The princess lost a key years ago. I suggest you have it.'

'She did lose a key; yes. But there are six other people in this house. I repeat, the filing cabinet was open.'

Once again there was a curious, suspended silence. Miss Pentecost looked strange; as if she was quite unreasonably afraid, and Simone watched her while answering Maria. 'Then we'll go and tell the princess now.'

'No.' Maria began calmly to replace the files, and took the sheets of flimsy from Miss Pentecost. 'The principessa is resting and cannot be disturbed; she is already much too excited. Tomorrow if you wish. Indeed I shall insist that we have an explanation tomorrow. You have become very important very quickly in this house, signorina, but still you cannot be allowed to insult others; even if they are merely servants.'

For the first time Simone raised her voice. 'Nonsense!' She switched suddenly to Miss Pentecost. 'Weeks ago you told me that Arturo thought there was something odd about Simonetta Vespucci's death. How did you know?'

Miss Pentecost moistened her lips with the tip of her tongue. 'Why ... I can't remember. Surely from Becky.' She added, 'Or someone else. Everybody's heard about Arturo's theories. If anyone cares.'

'This I don't understand,' Maria complained. 'First you accuse me of something; if one knew what. You then talk of Signor Vespucci. To me it seems confused.' She closed the cabinet with a crash, locked it and took out the key. 'I shall give this to the principessa.'

Simone said, 'It doesn't much matter now. But there's something going on in this house, something between the two of you, and I'd be a fool not to guess it's to do with the relics. You wouldn't be planning to steal them, I suppose?'

'That is quite, quite ridiculous,' Miss Pentecost whispered.

'And impossible,' Simone agreed. 'Because I know too much about you; at least I could suggest some very odd questions to the police. Your name, Maria, and your connection with that man Vespe; you gave that away the other morning when I mentioned him. When you read Arturo Vespucci's papers, Miss Pentecost, as much as you could read; and what you have to do with a person named d'Espinal—who absolutely refuses to talk about you.' She paused, watching both of them, and asked, 'Or is it blackmail. Because you know those things are stolen property? I can spoil that for you too, you know.'

'You can spoil nothing,' Maria started, but checked herself and finished, 'There is nothing to spoil. If you have something clear against us, against me, say so.'

'The first thing,' Simone told her coldly, 'is a letter. One came for me several days ago. Where is it?'

She was certain that Maria relaxed. The maid cried, 'Dear God, now you speak of that. Of course you have a right to be angry, and I am most truly sorry. There was indeed a letter and I put it aside to give to you; but one has so many things to think about. It will still be in the staff parlour.' The dark eyes became calculating suddenly. 'I shall send it at once; to your room.'

Miss Pentecost moved. She murmured, 'It's nearly eight o'clock; we should go and change,' and without looking at Simone went past them quickly and opened the door.

Maria watched her leave expressionlessly and then said, 'That is quite true, signorina; you will be very late and I must go to the principessa. Let us not spoil the reception for her, please.' She went to the door herself and finished, 'I am very sad about this. But if you will wait for only a few minutes in your room before starting to dress I shall send one of the men up with your letter.'

D'Espinal settled the Botticelli tenderly in the case, placing felt pads to protect it, and looked at his watch. He had done well, five minutes less than he had told Maria; it was not yet five to eight. Glancing again at the emeralds, on the small table under the easel, he pushed the curtains aside and stepped out over the scarlet silk guard rope to survey the empty reception salon, the banks of flowers, the tall windows with velvet drapes, and the elegant chairs arranged around the walls. It was a big room, but by nine thirty it would be crowded, and he ought not to have much difficulty about finding some corner from which to watch Maria and Miss Pentecost.

Hearing a voice from behind the closed doors he stiffened suddenly, but then a woman laughed too and he relaxed again; stepping back into the alcove he took up the picture case and passed silently through the wall door, closing it carefully behind him. The problem now was to convince Maria, if she checked, that he had left the house. That damned woman was sharp. She had remarked on his clothes at once and he suspected that she had only been half satisfied by his austere answer, that he personally never appeared anywhere after six thirty unless wearing a dinner jacket and black tie.

From this point on his own plans were fluid; he had worked out the broad objective, as it were—which was simply to possess himself also of the emeralds and whatever else was in that safe—but not yet his precise tactics. Since Maria had insisted that he must leave the house by eight o'clock it was possible that she was about some stratagem of her own unknown to Miss Pentecost; and presumably with the fellow Vespe. Clearly there was something less than perfect faith between the two ladies. But there was no reason why he should not at least appear to satisfy both of them; especially since it would encourage them each to proceed innocently with her own separate device.

He went down the steps behind the salon and out into the lower passage. Everything was still quiet and he moved on along to the porter's lodge just as silently himself. In here when Maria admitted him he had noticed a stack of surplus folding tables piled against one wall, and now he slipped the picture down carefully behind them; if she came this far she would be looking for him, not the Botticelli. Then, going out again, he unbolted the courtyard door and pulled it back a few inches. It was a detail; but it should persuade her that he had gone.

Turning back he paused at the other door opposite the lodge. This was ajar too, and he pushed it a little wider to peer inside. From the lingering vinous smell he judged it had once been a wine cellar, and in the dim light he could just make out a further door still, also open, at the far end. But there was nothing here of interest; his business now lay in the inhabited part of the house, familiarizing himself with its main corridors, so that he could follow Maria or Miss Pentecost without hesitation, or leave unobtrusively himself if necessary. He went on to the other passage which, as he remembered from his last visit, led up to the first floor and then on to the private apartments. Once there he was unlikely to be challenged. The women would now be dressing and the staff about their evening meal; even if some servant did become inquisitive he could depend on his natural manner of majesty and authority to carry him through.

Maria was breathless, but her eyes were vicious. She said, 'It must be now; at once.'

Staring down at the letter which she had thrust into his hands Vespe asked, 'But how do I do it?'

'With all your experience? Listen, you fool,' Maria whispered. 'It's you or her.' They were standing under the archway on the second floor corridor, and she glanced back one way towards Becky's suite and then the other to Simone's. 'Listen,' she repeated. 'The service entrance lies exactly opposite her rooms. This you must open to be ready. You then knock at her door and enter, and close it behind you; carefully. You will be extremely polite and give her the letter. I think she will open it at once. And when she does...' Maria shrugged. 'That is your affair. Only do not make a noise.'

'It's dangerous,' Vespe muttered.

'Not so dangerous as she is. The other man has left by now; he will not linger here once he has the picture. There is only the principessa on this floor and I shall see that she does not come out. But you must be quiet with it.'

Vespe started to say something again, but at that moment Mrs Teestock appeared from Becky's room. She bore down on them saying, 'Ah, Maria; there you are. The principessa is asking for you; it's getting late and she's a little annoyed.'

Maria sighed. 'These extra men are so stupid,' she complained, 'and there is so much to do.'

'It is trying,' Mrs Teestock agreed, 'but it will soon be over now.' She smiled soothingly, studied Vespe for a moment looking faintly puzzled, and turned up the stairs to the next floor.

Maria waited until she had gone and then breathed, 'Now go about it. And see that it is soon over.'

Waiting for Mrs Teestock in their own room Miss Pentecost thought fast and rather desperately. She admitted to herself that she was uneasy. Those things had a dreadful history; and there was no doubt now that Simone Greenwood might cause trouble. But she told herself that no rational person need be superstitious about something which had happened so long ago, and whatever Greenwood suspected she still had no proof; she would be talking in a climate of disbelief from the beginning, and even if she did persuade the police to start enquiries it could be days or weeks before they got anywhere. Maria would of course deny any connection with the man Vespe; and it was more than possible that since the relics were stolen property anyhow even Becky would be careful of going too far.

It would all be a little more difficult perhaps, a little more risky; but they must go on. In any case it was too late to stop; d'Espinal would already have the picture by now. But there were two things certain. Judith must not be allowed to know anything about Greenwood's suspicions, and she herself must watch Maria; if, as d'Espinal said, Vespe really was in Venice it became obvious that they were planning something between them.

Mrs Teestock came in then, and with a look which Miss Pentecost recognized at once; it usually meant that Judith had finally made up her mind. She said to herself, 'Oh God, I hope we're not going through it all again,' but asked, 'Darling, where have you been? It's getting very late.'

'Talking to Becky,' Mrs Teestock answered shortly. 'I went down to see how she was and found her most upset because Maria seemed to have disappeared.'

'Maria's here and everywhere tonight. She's thoroughly enjoying the excuse to be even more efficient than usual. Did you find her?'

'A minute ago. She was whispering to a very peculiar looking waiter at one of the service doors; I had a most unpleasant impression.' Mrs Teestock paused and then went on abruptly, 'Emilia, I've decided we must stop this.'

'Judith,' Miss Pentecost protested. 'Not again, please.'

'Again; and this time finally. It's strange, but I've discovered I'm quite fond of poor Becky. She's as excited as a child, and I just will not see her hurt in this way. She was telling me what she means to do with the relics; and I agree with her.' Mrs Teestock stopped once more and then said, 'She told me the whole story. I never dreamed of anything so horrible.'

'But that was all so long ago,' Miss Pentecost protested.

'Then you know it too?'

'I read Miss Greenwood's report.'

'And you're still prepared to go on? Don't you realize that we're involving ourselves in sacrilege and murder?'

'My dear, we're not responsible for that.'

'We're making ourselves accessories to it. I don't agree with Becky when she says there's a curse on those things, that's too fanciful; but I want no part of them myself. I must warn you, Emilia, that if you go on and anything happens tonight I shall tell Becky everything I know.'

It was getting dusky in the room and Miss Pentecost moved across to switch on the lights, to gain time to think. There must be a way round this, but for the present it was best apparently to give in to Judith. She needed to talk to d'Espinal, and said, 'Very well, my dear; if that's what you want. But we've left it late now. D'Espinal will already have the portrait.'

'Then he must put it back.' Mrs Teestock spoke as if that would be quite simple. 'I've no doubt you know what his arrangements are. And you must stop Maria. Unless I'm much mistaken the person she was talking to was the man who shot that poor old nun. Becky told me about him.'

'Vespe?' Miss Pentecost stared at her. 'Vespe's

here? Are you sure of that?'

'This man was certainly not a waiter; and with two fingers missing from his hand he fits Becky's description. Maria was whispering to him most urgently. She was giving him a letter.'

Miss Pentecost remembered suddenly a fleeting look on Maria's face only a few minutes ago in the study; remembered also a note in her voice days before when she remarked, 'So we must think of something for Miss Greenwood'. She realized now that the menace had been there even then; and that she had chosen deliberately not to see it. A sudden wave of pure fear swept over her, but Mrs Teestock was watching rather curiously and she forced herself to say, 'It may not mean anything; all the same, he ought not to be here. Maria will be with Becky, but I'll have the house searched for him. And I'll tell d'Espinal.' Looking back from the door she added carefully, 'And Aunt Judith; I think you might go down and see whether Miss Greenwood needs anything. I promised I'd look in myself.'

'I must take an aspirin first,' Mrs Teestock said. 'I think I've got one of my headaches coming on. You see what I mean?' she asked. 'It's so easy to start things. It's keeping them under control which gets difficult.'

Miss Pentecost edged out of the alcove in the salon and started back once more for the porter's lodge. D'Espinal had changed the pictures but there was no other trace of him; why was he not waiting for her as he had promised? And that was quite obvious, she thought bitterly, fumbling and slipping down the steps again. Because he had gone; because he had cheated her as she might have known he would; as she had cheated herself by imagining that she could always manage other people.

Hurrying into the lodge again she stared round as if, miraculously, she might see something which she had not noticed before; but it remained just as silent and empty as it was five minutes ago. She knew now that all their plans were finished, but that was not so painful as the thought of d'Espinal tricking her; and even that was less than her sudden awful responsibility for Greenwood. Standing there she asked herself desperately what Maria would do. They would try to get her out of the house, of course; but they could not take her by the front entrance, where there were already people waiting to watch the guests arrive, so they must bring her this way. She herself could either go back and have the building searched for Vespe or wait here for whatever was to happen. The first was impossible because Becky would inevitably want to know why; and the second was asking too much. That man was a violent brute and he would be fighting for his own freedom.

She looked at her wristlet watch. It was eight fifteen—everything had happened so quickly—and she said, 'Perhaps Harcourt will come after all, I must wait until half past at least; Judith must be with Greenwood by now...' Then she heard a whisper of sound; someone coming down the steps and a door creaking open. With a wild hope that it might be d'Espinal at last she started out into the passage but stopped again, frozen, listening to the heavy footsteps and a low, harsh voice cursing in Italian. She stood there for a moment, almost until it was too late, before drawing back into the lodge to switch off the light and wait.

The house was bigger than d'Espinal had thought, but he was satisfied now that by using any of the service passages—all of which had at least one entrance on each floor—he would have no difficulty in making a discreet exit when he had finally possessed himself of the emeralds and whatever else was in that safe. 'An admirable arrangement,' he told himself complacently; 'I begin to feel I have a talent for this kind of thing.'

So far he had seen only one servant, and she had shown no interest in him; and apart from nearly being discovered by Maria, who had chosen suddenly to peer out along the corridor from the princess's private apartment, there had been no other mishaps. Speculating curiously on the maid's somewhat furtive manner he had just managed to edge behind the hanging tapestry of an archway in time. But he had judged that it would be well to examine the first floor corridors and the entrance to the salon and then retreat to the porter's lodge to wait for Miss Pentecost. It was important still, he considered, to keep Miss Pentecost happy.

But here, as he admitted philosophically, the tide of fortune turned against him. He was starting down the between floor stairs when a youngish fellow, apparently an under footman from his striped waistcoat, appeared at the foot of them. He stood aside politely for d'Espinal to descend, but there was no mistaking the curiosity, even a touch of suspicion on his face. 'Pardon me, signore...' he started.

'Of course,' d'Espinal murmured. 'Is there something?'

'You are clearly not of the staff, signore,' the young man suggested. 'And the guests have not yet started to arrive.'

D'Espinal nodded benevolently. 'There you have a point, an excellent point'; and a damned awkward point, he thought. He asked, 'What is your name?'

'Alberto, signore,' the footman answered.

At the same moment d'Espinal heard footsteps coming down the upper stairs and turning along the corridor above; moving slightly to listen, thinking it would be still more damned awkward if any of the women came out and discovered him, he said, 'You will wish to know who I am; naturally.'

'Of your pleasure, signore.' Alberto was courteous, but uncompromisingly firm.

Up there someone tapped on a door insistently; and then Mrs Teestock's clear and rather penetrating voice called, 'Miss Greenwood, are you there?' There was silence again and d'Espinal leaned forward impressively. 'In a word,' he whispered, 'Security.'

'Security, signore?' Alberto enquired. At the same time the footsteps moved on; still Mrs Teestock apparently, now tapping at another door and then asking, 'Maria, is Miss Greenwood with the principessa?'

'It cannot have escaped your notice,' d'Espinal breathed heavily, 'that there are treasures of incalculable value to be exhibited tonight.' He could not hear the other voice, but he caught Mrs Teestock saying, 'No, Becky, there's nothing wrong; I'm only looking for Miss Greenwood.' She added, 'In the old study, Maria? She should be dressing by now; I'll go down and remind her of the time.'

'Security from where, signore?' the intolerable young man asked. 'We have heard nothing of this.'

'For a very good reason,' d'Espinal told him shortly. 'The principessa does not wish my presence known.'

'Perhaps,' Alberto suggested, 'you should come to Signor Luciano, our butler.'

Mrs Teestock was still talking; but finally she called, 'Don't worry, Becky, I'll see she's not late,' and the footsteps approached along the corridor again. D'Espinal said, 'Young man, I have no time for social niceties'; and no time to be seen by Mrs Teestock either, he added to himself. There was a service door in the panelling barely six feet away and he moved towards it firmly, finishing, 'My business is to examine the rear entrance to this building immediately; to see that all is safe there.'

'Then I shall come with you,' Alberto said. 'And we will go to Signor Luciano afterwards.'

'Do so by all means,' d'Espinal answered between his teeth. 'If you have no more pressing duties.' With something less than his customary urbanity he pushed past Alberto and opened the door, catching a fleeting glimpse of Mrs Teestock turning from the stairs as they entered. Resisting an evil impulse to pitch this pertinacious young pest bodily down the steps he said, 'You may lead the way.'

He would have to depend upon Miss Pentecost now. She was a woman with some modicum of intelligence and doubtless known to this fellow; given a hint she would corroborate his own story readily enough. He must be from the British Consulate, he thought.

The idea pleased him. He had always nursed a secret desire to be a man of the Consular or Diplomatic Services; he considered himself to be eminently suitable for either.

She imagined it was hours, although it could scarcely have been more than seconds. A shadow came first over the flagstones, and then what appeared to be one of the waiters, incongruous in the respectable black uniform, white shirt front and bow tie, with a diamond flashing on one hand. Puffing slightly and sweating with the effort he was carrying Simone Greenwood like a limp rag doll half over his shoulder; Miss Pentecost caught her breath harshly, pressing one hand to her mouth to stop herself screaming, feeling the knuckles painfully against her teeth. He approached the door on the other side of the passage and pushed it open with his foot to swing the girl through. Then Miss Pentecost heard him stumbling inside and whispered suddenly, 'I can't!' It sounded so loud that she thought Vespe must have heard but there was no answer from the cellar and, taking one deep breath, she edged out to the passage, stopping there again and looking back along it; telling herself desperately that there was nothing she could do alone, she could get all the help she needed in a few minutes.

'A few minutes...' she whispered and went on into the wine cellar. Still carrying Simone, Vespe now seemed to have several keys in one hand, fumbling at a further door with absolute blackness beyond it, and Miss Pentecost thought with a curious sort of detachment that he would probably kill both of them, lock them both away down here. Once more she had an almost irresistible impulse to turn back, race up into the house and scream for help; but then she thought Simone moved suddenly. She heard Vespe curse again, saw him twist one hand round to clamp it over the girl's mouth, and she herself screamed, 'Stop that.' Something rolled away from her foot, a bottle clinking across the stone flags, while Vespe jerked his head round, his face fixed and eyes glittering in the light from the passage as Miss Pentecost launched herself at him.

She had a momentary glimpse of Simone, released and slipping helplessly to the ground, and then everything seemed to explode into violence. Somehow she clung to Vespe, clawing and kicking, swearing breathlessly herself and now reckless with fury. He was panting and out of condition but still too strong for her and she screamed again, either with rage or fear, before he flung her back at the wall. She seemed to jar and hang for a long time before crumpling down on to her knees, seeing Vespe's arm raised and waiting for it to fall.

But it stopped short and from somewhere a voice boomed, 'What is this?' There was a clatter of echoing footsteps and the cellar filled suddenly with shadows; another man was cursing in Italian and d'Espinal roared, 'At him, boy!' Shaking her head angrily, Miss Pentecost's vision cleared. She saw Alberto locked against Vespe, d'Espinal standing prudently aside but circling with them and clutching a dusty bottle at arm's length, and closed her eyes again; but heard d'Espinal call, 'Hold him steady, boy!' heard a sharp ringing crack and a grunt. Everything seemed to be very quiet then until she realized that she was crouching ridiculously, leaning on her hands and peering up at d'Espinal; she said defensively, 'I did my best.'

'What the devil was he about?' d'Espinal demanded.

'Isn't it obvious?' Pushing herself upright she took in Alberto, now bending over Simone; Vespe lying grotesquely on his back with his mouth open, white shirt front bulging and his respectable bow tie twisted under one ear. 'He was going to shut her away down here somewhere.'

Looking from her to Vespe and then at the open door and the tunnel beyond it, d'Espinal snapped authoritatively, 'Wait,' and disappeared, while she watched Simone now staring at Alberto uncertainly and putting up one hand to push the hair out of her eyes. Alberto was muttering viciously and, surprised to find her own voice so firm suddenly, Miss Pentecost told him, 'Don't fuss, Alberto; she'll be all right.'

D'Espinal came back quickly, glancing down at Vespe again; he said, 'Get her out of here; and you, Alberto, help me dispose of this animal.' Miss Pentecost asked, 'What...?' and he went on, 'Get her up to her room, see what you can do for her, and wait for me.' Alberto too started to speak, but he roared again, 'By God I will not have this questioning; do as you're told. Can you stand?' he asked Simone.

'Of course I can,' she answered irritably. 'I've just got a stiff neck. What's been happening? And what're you doing here? I knew there was something funny...'

'It doesn't matter,' Miss Pentecost cut in. 'An accident. If we don't go now you'll be late for the reception.' With one arm round Simone's shoulders, saying, 'Don't worry now,' but thinking that the girl was still a nuisance she led her out to the passage. Behind them she heard d'Espinal say grimly, 'Now Alberto...' and then the sound of a limp, heavy body dragged over the pavestones.

She was waiting outside Simone's door when, only a few minutes later, d'Espinal emerged from the service door with Alberto. Returned to his normal manner he announced, 'You have done excellently well, young man. Remember now; not a word to a soul, my good fellow, and I shall see to it personally that the principessa hears all about you.' Then, waiting for Alberto to leave, he asked Miss Pentecost, 'Well? How is she?'

Miss Pentecost laughed raggedly. 'Very annoyed. But she doesn't seem to have taken any harm. Apparently the last thing she remembers is Vespe bringing her a letter and starting to read it. And she insists on being at the reception. Judith's with her, helping her to dress; Judith's rather good in an emergency.' She took a deep breath and asked, 'What do we do now? Even apart from this trouble with Miss Greenwood I must tell you that Judith's turned very difficult. She's decided that it's all too unkind to Becky. And it seems that those things...' Miss Pentecost corrected herself. 'The picture really does have a rather dreadful history. Judith says if you don't put the portrait back she'll tell Becky everything.'

For a moment an extraordinarily wolfish look passed over d'Espinal's face. 'Mrs Teestock appears to be a lady who does not know her own mind.'

'This time she does. Only too well.'

'And what is yours?'

She hesitated. 'I'm not sure.'

'Then I will tell you mine. We continue. Because there is something more in that safe which is clearly part of your stratagem with Maria.'

'How d'you know that?' Miss Pentecost whispered.

'My remarkably acute intelligence. Your own evasions and mistakes. Your statement the other day that the real emeralds would be in the safe whereas they are to be exhibited with the portrait. The fact that your part is to purloin those emeralds while Maria for some reason is to possess herself of the safe and alarm keys. It points to only one conclusion. That at some time tonight you or Maria or both of you propose to open that safe and remove whatever else is left. A clean sweep, as it were, dear Emilia. What is it?' he demanded.

She started, 'You...' and then finished, 'a breviary.'

He looked at her reproachfully. 'And you thought never to tell me? Very well then. You will proceed exactly as planned; as I am convinced that Maria will even if you do not.'

'She won't do it. It's impossible now.'

'To Maria nothing is impossible. She dare not ask questions about Vespe so you need not answer any. As to Miss Greenwood you may say that Alberto discovered her lying at the foot of the service steps. Listen Emilia; Vespe is now incarcerated in a sort of dungeon or oubliette down there. And by the time I have finished with Maria she will be glad enough to disappear too; I may even allow her to release Vespe. Do you not see the inference if they and all of the Vespucci relics vanish alike?'

'It's possible, I suppose. But Judith?'

'When faced with the fact Mrs Teestock will doubtless see it sensibly. Most people do.'

'I'm not so sure that she will. And if I refuse myself?'

'If you refuse the portrait at least will go; only I know where that is at present. And we shall not meet in Milan.' Since they were not likely to in any case, he thought, that scarcely mattered; but it made a good bargaining point.

She studied him for a moment and said, 'You're a swine.'

'I am as God made me,' he told her modestly. 'Remember that I still want the provenance of the portrait too. I gather Miss Greenwood made some kind of discovery.'

'She did indeed.' Miss Pentecost looked uneasy again. 'I can tell you now.'

'We have no time,' he interrupted. 'You have barely half an hour to array yourself for the reception. I shall see you there. For the present I propose to find some quiet corner and wait for my own entrance.' She stared at him blankly and he explained, 'My dear, does it not occur to you that when you open that safe you also may stand in some need of protection from Maria? I shall be at hand.'

CHAPTER TEN

D'Espinal had entered the salon majestically but unnoticed simply by passing behind several other guests while the somewhat flustered Luciano was announcing them. He was now standing in one of the windows, not precisely concealed nor yet openly advertising himself, watching the princess and Simone. The girl looked pale but determined, undoubtedly a tough little creature; and Mrs Teestock had performed a remarkable job in getting the young person fully recovered and presentable in such short order. Which disproved the legend, d'Espinal considered, that all ladies invariably require an eternity in which to dress.

Clearly also none of them had said anything to alarm the princess. At this moment, he judged, she was supremely happy; pleasantly excited, carrying herself with a small regality not entirely devoid of an amusing touch of malice. One felt unaccountably drawn towards her, and for a moment he reflected that he would infinitely sooner be selling her a picture than purloining one from her. Pentecost was a small nagging worry too; he could not conceal from himself the fact that what he proposed—in the vulgar tongue, to ditch her—was a damned dirty dog's trick; even Paolo had seemed to grow curiously remote that afternoon in the garden when listening to his final plans. But by involving him in this stratagem she had shown no particular consideration for his own finer feelings, and she would get over it eventually; '"It is a merciful provision in nature,"' he quoted to himself, '"that time hath an art to heal the smartest strokes of affliction".'

Listening amiably to the orchestra discoursing a selection from Rosenkavalier he accepted a glass of champagne from a passing waiter, now observing Maria enter and pass discreetly behind the princess and Simone, apparently here only to supervise the service. She too was a remarkable person, and he wondered briefly who had ever put the superstition around that women were the weaker sex. Although on seeing Simone here tonight she must have realized that something had gone awry she showed no sign of fear or hesitation. He was certain that with or without Vespe, perhaps better without him, Maria would continue with her own arrangements. It all hung now on Emilia Pentecost; and Mrs Teestock.

He heard Luciano's sad voice announcing them then. They came in, to pause by the princess and Simone; Mrs Teestock asking something of the girl, who laughed and shook her head. Nevertheless in spite of the social graces of the moment there would be questions tomorrow, a general raising of the devil if he read that character too; but they would be questions to which there were no answers. More people were following the San Giorgio ladies in and they moved on; Mrs Teestock nodding to faces in the thickening crowd, stopping to speak to others, and Miss Pentecost glancing round with a trace of tension obviously looking for himself. Then she caught his eye and came across quickly. He murmured, 'You're late.'

'Obviously. There were things to do while Judith was dressing.' She added, 'Maria suspects something; wants to know why you're still here.'

'Tell her that I've changed my plans but all is well. You have the emeralds?' Miss Pentecost nodded, showing him the velvet dress bag she was carrying, and he went on, 'And Miss Greenwood's report?'

'I had to take a copy from Becky's room.' She produced a few tightly folded sheets of flimsy from the same bag. 'That's the press hand out, but it tells you quite enough. You'd better read it now. You might understand what's worrying Judith.'

'Later. What time do you start your operation with Maria?'

'Half past nine. She comes through to the buffet and I follow her.'

D'Espinal looked at his watch. It was then nine twenty-five and he murmured, 'Then I shall move on at once.'

'You're insane, you know,' Miss Pentecost whispered. 'Perhaps Becky's right; perhaps there is something about those things...'

But without hurrying and carefully avoiding Mrs Teestock, who was now talking earnestly to an austere but important looking priest, he was already edging his way through the crowd towards the door. As he reached it Luciano announced, 'The Signora Messina-Silvestro, the Dottore Arcado Venturi,' and he waited curiously for them to come in. An iron grey woman with an imperious manner and a hawk nose, and a small man who resembled nothing so much as an evil tempered cockatoo in a dinner jacket, even to his crest of yellowish white hair

D'Espinal paused to watch the daggers of dislike between the two ladies, Mrs Messina-Silvestro's cold appraising stare at Simone while the extraordinary little man bowed and chattered and sidled exactly like a parrot again, and then slipped out adroitly.

In the hall more people were flooding up from the entrance floor, Alberto and one other footman standing there to marshall them on. It was a pretty scene d'Espinal considered, reminiscent of the elegant days of old Venice; the bright dresses and sober black jackets, even a sprinkling of uniforms. But he did not linger to admire it. He waited only until Alberto became engaged with a fresh group and then moved on into the main corridor and out of sight up the stairs. Two more minutes and he was in the princess's sitting-room.

The lights were still on showing the blank wall from which the picture had been taken, with the panel flat back and covering the safe. For the present that did not interest him; he judged the alarms would still be alive. His immediate concern was some place of concealment and he crossed over to the other doorway which, as he expected from his first visit, opened into a large and ornate bedroom. In here he satisfied himself with a single swift look round and then switched off all the lamps and closed the door carefully to a few inches; leaving only a clear view of the empty wall, one end of the roll top desk, and a pretty little ormolu clock which now said nine thirty-two.

He had little more than another minute to wait. From his position d'Espinal did not see them come in, but he heard the outer door open and close softly. Maria said, 'We must be quick. I feel there is something wrong. What happened with this girl? There was no time to ask Alberto.'

'I don't know,' Miss Pentecost answered. 'Apparently neither does she. He found her at the bottom of the service steps. She must have been following someone and fallen down them.'

D'Espinal nodded approvingly. He breathed, 'Bravo, Emilia.'

'Who was it?' Maria demanded. 'Did she say?'

'I told you; she doesn't know. Does it matter?'

'Where are the emeralds?' Maria asked.

Miss Pentecost said, 'When you've opened the safe.'

They were quiet for a few seconds until Maria whispered, 'There, that is the alarm,' and laughed. 'It was so simple. The poor old woman will not wear her spectacles, and I tell her "Madame, you must take care with those" and place two little car keys in her dress bag.'

'You must remember to change them back.'

'Of course.' Maria sounded slightly contemptuous. 'Neither shall I forget the signorina's papers.'

They came into d'Espinal's line of vision suddenly, Maria holding what did in fact look like a silver ignition key. She glanced back at the bedroom door, perhaps still expecting to see Vespe in there, as d'Espinal was convinced she had planned; she was puzzled, he thought, but still confident, and he understood suddenly that she really did imagine she was the true mistress of this house and everything in it.

Swinging the panel aside to show a small square depression let into the wall she slipped the key into a minute slot, turned it, and opened the safe. Miss

Pentecost watched silently while she reached into the cavity behind and brought out a package folded in wash leather; holding it in her two hands for a moment she whispered, 'After so long, when Stefan himself could not do it,' before carrying it to the desk and opening up the wrapping. D'Espinal caught a glint of gold and precious stones, heard Miss Pentecost catch her breath sharply while Maria went on, 'I have only seen this once before, when I was quite a small girl in my mother's house. But even then I knew that one day it would belong to me.'

He stepped out quietly. Both women were oblivious to everything except the Book of Hours of Simonetta Vespucci lying on the desk, gleaming softly against the glitter of her emerald necklace. 'You do understand?' Maria asked. 'This is mine.'

D'Espinal answered, 'Not yet, Maria. Not ever.' It was then nine thirty-seven and he went on, 'We have a little time, but not much; and I propose to give you your instructions, Maria.'

Back in the porter's lodge Miss Pentecost said. 'I'm coming with you.'

It was a damned nuisance that she was down here at all, he thought; the next few minutes were likely to be somewhat delicate. But his conscience was still uneasy about Emilia and he answered gently enough, 'That would be most unwise. You must stay for a few days; to persuade Mrs Teestock to see the light, as it were.'

'She won't, you know,' Miss Pentecost told him desperately. 'Harcourt, now we've done it I'm afraid.'

He was already opening out the wash leather for just one glimpse of the breviary before leaving and he argued, 'You've no need to be; and don't you see what it will look like if you also disappear along with Spoletti and Vespe and these things?' but then stopped suddenly.

Even in the dim light it blazed. The cover was worked gold set with pearls and cabuchon emeralds, with an inset in enamels portraying the device of Pallas Athene carried by Giuliano de' Medici on his personal banner in the Great Tournament. On the first leaf there was an inscription which d'Espinal whispered in rough translation; "To the all conquering Queen of Love from that son of Mars she has vanquished; Anno 1476; made for Giuliano de' M. by S.B." Under it was written, "I pray that in some measure the contemplation of this following may bring you joy, and to recover your precious strength."

There followed pages of exquisite Italian script and, opposite each, a tiny glowing picture appropriate to the month of the year; every one still as warm and brilliant as it must have been on the day it was painted. D'Espinal stared at them unbelievingly. So far as he knew—and that, stripped of all self-conceit, was almost as much as could be known—there was no record that Sandro Botticelli had ever attempted miniatures. But his hand was here. You could see it in all the allegories, already hints of Primavera and the Birth of Venus, in the stylised sensuousness and every subtlety of line and colour. This book was unique; by some, he thought, it might be considered superior even to the Grimani Breviary or the Very Rich Hours of the Duc de Berry.

And, coming down to more earthly considerations, immensely valuable. Easily portable and easily hidden, easily saleable, above all easily authenticated; indeed it carried its own authentication. There was not a great library on earth which would not be prepared to bid for it; and not a few, he suspected, would be ready to accept it without asking too many questions. He whispered, 'Dear loving God.'

'Have you read that press notice?' Miss Pentecost demanded.

'Not yet,' he answered absently. 'There'll be time for that. Will you open the courtyard door? Paolo Raffaele will be waiting,' he explained. 'I promised he should see these before I left.'

'You're impossible,' she told him. 'You're out of your mind.'

But he was already taking the portrait out of its case and she turned away helplessly. Left to himself he breathed, 'I am unworthy; they almost frighten even me,' but when Miss Pentecost came back with the older man he said, 'One brief glimpse, Paolo; it's a pity, old friend, but I must be away. Is Andreas here with the boat?'

'The boat?' Miss Pentecost asked sharply. 'What for?'

D'Espinal again felt that uneasy twinge of conscience, but he said, 'To the station, Emilia; by the least frequented canals.' In fact the boat was to take him to Mestre where there would be a hired car to drive him north towards the Alps and the frontier.

Paolo nodded. 'Andreas is waiting for you.'

He was studying the treasures expressionlessly and d'Espinal asked, 'Come, Paolo, don't you have anything to say?' watching while his old friend turned the pages of the breviary delicately with his finger tips, aware suddenly that for the first time in all the years they had known each other Paolo Raffaele was against him. 'Paolo,' he went on almost pleadingly. 'There's never been anything like them before. Dear God, that I should be so privileged.'

Paolo looked round at him. 'You call it privileged? To be a common thief?'

'No,' d'Espinal protested. 'Not a common thief. There's nothing common about those things.'

'A thief nevertheless. What will you do with them?'

'Five million dollars,' d'Espinal said. 'At least.'

'And what can you get with it which you don't have already? Or what will you lose? I must tell you that you would never be welcome in my house afterwards.'

D'Espinal was reproachful again. 'That's unkind. I could keep them,' he suggested hopefully.

'You'd drive yourself mad; wanting to show them to people and never daring to do so.'

'Are you both against me?' d'Espinal asked sadly.

'You're against yourself,' Paolo told him and Miss Pentecost cut in, 'Harcourt, before you do anything, read that report; and you too, Signore Raffaele. We don't have much time.'

D'Espinal said, 'Very well,' and took the few sheets of flimsy from his pocket, flattening them on the table. It was quiet again except for the rustle of paper as he flipped over each page, Miss Pentecost watching them both steadily, but at last d'Espinal straightened up and murmured, 'Yes; I see. It makes one think.'

He looked at Miss Pentecost and she told him, 'If you go, I shall come with you. Or if you take them back we might just be in time. They're dangerous, Harcourt; they always will be.'

'Take them back,' Paolo added. 'If you don't ... I

must tell you that if you leave this house with them, Harcourt, I shall call the Chief of Police at once. You'll never get those things out of Italy.'

D'Espinal sighed heavily. He said, 'You ask a great deal, but so be it. I shall carry the picture, Emilia; you the breviary and necklace. And we can only pray for inspiration. But first...' He tossed a heavy key on to the table with a clatter. 'You will recollect I said I should leave that, Emilia. It might even help us now. Let us go, then.'

When they reached the hall Luciano and the waiters, the other footmen and Alberto, were grouped around the salon doors peering in; there was a fragmented murmur of voices and above it one saying loudly, 'An impudent fraud,' and another—still with an extraordinary resemblance to a parrot in it—chattering, 'No more a Botticelli than I am. Then Mrs Teestock appeared, pushing through the men, her face white and shocked; seeing Miss Pentecost and d'Espinal there she stopped suddenly, staring at them for a moment before bearing down on them quickly and saying, 'Emilia, I told you; I warned you. If you could have seen what it was like in there...' She stopped again and asked, 'What is this? What are you doing now?'

'What does it look like, madame?' d'Espinal demanded. 'We have foiled an impudent plot to make off with these priceless treasures and are now about to restore them to the Princess Kodaly. And if you are wise,' he added softly, 'you will follow my lead and corroborate everything I say. Alberto...' he called, 'a moment, if you please.'

Alberto said, 'Signore, it's bad; I could kill them.

They're laughing at her.'

'Not for much longer. Listen, young man. In a few minutes you will be a hero; and you'll be asked questions by the newspapers. You will tell them that we left the man Vespe lying, and he must have made his escape. You understand? Do that and listen to what I have to say in there, and I personally promise that the principessa will see you set up for life... And now, ladies, let us have an end to this. "De l'audace, encore de l'audace, et toujours de l'audace." And God help us if we don't tell a good story.'

Inside the salon there was a tight crowd around the alcove, whispering and watching; on the orchestra rostrum the musicians, still clutching their instruments, were stretching up to peer. One woman giggled; Becky said tiredly, 'Let be, love; tell 'em to go home,' and Simone's voice came over clearly and angrily, 'I will not let be. I say the real portrait's been stolen; and the emeralds.' One of the men laughed and Simone demanded furiously, 'Stop that. I know who arranged it, and we shall call the police.'

'The police?' This cold voice could only be Mrs Messina-Silvestro. 'A fine thing you'll do with the police, girl. The police know all about you. The whole of Venice knows all about you. Living on this foolish old woman, cheating her; even taking clothes from her. You should speak about the police; you'll be wiser to go back where you came from.'

'Leave that girl alone,' Becky screamed. 'What she is to me is my business.' But more of them were laughing and Simone herself snapped, 'I said, stop that.' She repeated, 'I tell you I know who arranged this and I want them now. Where is Mrs Judith Teestock? And Miss Pentecost?'

D'Espinal used the sudden quietness. He announced, 'They are here to answer for themselves.' Carrying the portrait, Emilia Pentecost with the breviary and emeralds, flanked by Mrs Teestock and Alberto, he advanced ponderously saying, 'Ladies and gentlemen, make way if you please.' Reaching the princess—red faced and tear stained but now with a light of Yorkshire fury in her eyes—he went on, 'Madame; I have the honour of restoring to you these beautiful and precious relics, of which I believe you are the custodian.'

Becky clutched at Simone's arm, staring at the breviary. She whispered, 'Where did you get that?'

'It is a tale which I shall unfold.' Looking around his silent audience, enjoying every moment Miss Pentecost thought, 'I am Harcourt d'Espinal; a name which is not unknown in the world of historic art. I was called to Venice by the two devoted ladies of San Giorgio, because for some months past they have suspected the existence of a singularly cunning and deep-laid plot to purloin these treasures. In a word, they felt that my knowledge ..."' He looked down his nose modestly. 'My knowledge and vast experience were needed here.'

Smiling benevolently at Simone he continued, 'You will understand, Miss Greenwood, that some secrecy was unavoidable. First they did not wish to alarm their dear friend, the princess; second because I myself advised that it was best to allow this plot or stratagem to reach its climax and so have done with it for good. Tonight, madame,' he went on to Becky again, 'by the selfless efforts of these two ladies, the courage of this brave young man Alberto—whom I recommend to your attention—and my own not inconsiderable efforts we have reached this happy conclusion. I trust,' he asked, 'that we have the gentlemen of the press with us? At this stage a few photographs would be appropriate before I particularize our story.' Not only appropriate, indeed. They would give Maria time to get herself and Vespe out of the house; although one did not think she would linger.

'Larger than life,' Miss Pentecost said.

D'Espinal answered, 'It's so fatally easy to be smaller. It was an excellent tale, well told.' He gazed across benevolently at the knot of people still studying the picture—now guarded proudly by Alberto—closed his eyes to listen to the orchestra, and caught a snatch of conversation between the princess and Mrs Messina-Silvestro, who was clearly losing no time about hitching herself to the rising star.

It was crisp and still slightly acidulated. She was saying, 'Becky ... I can't call you by that ridiculous title,' and Becky told her, 'So far as I know nobody ever asked you to.' Mrs Silvestro acknowledged the riposte with a nod and continued, 'I shall want you on my committee; but I must warn you, it's expensive,' and then Becky answered, 'I daresay I can find the money; if I fancy it.' Not to be put down Mrs Silvestro turned her iron grey attention to Simone. 'And you, Miss Greenwood—I must apologize, I always admit when I'm wrong; it's so good for the soul—obviously have a brilliant future. I can arrange some most useful introductions for you. We must see you in Rome. Come and have tea tomorrow and we'll talk about it.' But Becky said, 'Not tomorrow. One of these days; we'll let you know.'

'How charming is renunciation,' d'Espinal murmured, 'when it produces sweetness and light.'

Mrs Teestock sniffed. 'Mrs Messina-Silvestro always moves fast; but she won't get far with Becky. I hope not because I must talk to her first; about my people on the islands. But for the present I still want to know about Maria.'

'Maria...' d'Espinal mused. 'She was a simple soul in the end. It appeared that she had met Stefan Kodaly years before in Zurich, where her precious Uncle Vespe was living and she herself then working for a Swiss family. Between them they concocted some scheme even then. As you know, they could never bring it off. But when the princess read this famous article about Miss Greenwood and you two ladies began to take an active interest...' He smiled at them gently. 'Stefan of course was dead, but Maria informed her dear uncle that the game was afoot again.'

Mrs Teestock eyed him suspiciously. 'And she herself told you all this?'

'Very easily and quickly. It was suggested that she too might be transferred to that oubliette or dungeon to keep company with Uncle Vespe. The thought seemed to distress her.' Miss Pentecost shivered and d'Espinal went on, 'Or there could be the police and charges of conspiracy and attempted murder by a particularly cruel and wicked method. Obviously, however, there was a danger that in this case she might talk about you two dear ladies and even myself. Probably the police would not believe her; they are sceptical by nature. But scandal is always distasteful and I offered her a third alternative. To leave this house by ten fifteen, removing her charming uncle with her; and thereafter to take care that neither of them should ever be seen or heard of again. I do not think they will.'

Mrs Teestock herself appeared to be listening to the music, and watching Doctor Venturi now bobbing and sidling to Simone. At last she murmured, 'We did enjoy planning it, at least.' She paused and then sighed and went on, 'I don't know what we shall do about San Giorgio. And you, Emilia.'

D'Espinal coughed delicately. 'I have a small proposition, madame; a thought which pleases me. Our dear Emilia has a gift for reproducing Old Masters; with a little training it might become a great gift. And I have considerable expertise in selling them. While you have an entirely delightful island which I should be delighted to consider as my second home. One can foresee a pleasant and most profitable partnership.'

Mrs Teestock considered that, now studying Mrs Messina-Silvestro and Becky, Venturi and Simone, all together about the portrait. 'I give them just one week before they start quarrelling again,' she observed. 'Why, yes, Mr d'Espinal; I should be delighted. And it would give poor Emilia something to do. That's what she really needs.'

Miss Pentecost said nothing.